Love and Mistletoe

A Beach Reads Holiday Contemporary Romance

~ Book V ~

The Summer Sisters Tame the Billionaires
Book Club Edition

Jean Oram

Oram Productions Alberta, Canada

This is a work of fiction and all characters, organizations, places, events, and incidents appearing in this novel are products of the author's active imagination or are used in a fictitious manner. Any resemblance to actual people, alive or dead, as well as any resemblance to events or locales, unless stated, is coincidental and, truly, a little bit cool.

LOVE AND MISTLETOE Copyright © 2015 by Jean Oram

All rights reserved, including the right to reproduce this book or portions thereof in any form whatsoever, unless written permission has been granted by the author, with the exception of brief quotations for use in a review of this work. For more information contact Jean Oram at JeanOramBooks@gmail.com. www.JeanOram.com

Printed in the United States of America unless otherwise stated on the last page of this book. Published by Oram Productions Alberta, Canada.

LIBRARY OF CONGRESS CATALOGING-IN-PUBLICATION DATA

Oram, Jean.
    Love and Mistletoe: A Beach Reads Holiday Contemporary Romance / Jean Oram.—1st. ed.
    p. cm.
    ISBN 978-1-928198-23-9 (paperback)
    Ebook ISBN 978-1-928198-24-6
1. Romance fiction. 2. Sisters—Fiction. 3. Firefighters—Fiction. 4. Romance fiction—Small towns. 5. Love stories, Canadian. 6. Small towns—Fiction. 7. Muskoka (Ont.)—Fiction. 8. Interpersonal relations—Fiction.

Summary: Simone Pascal, CEO of her own design company and honorary Summer Sister, is ready to start a family... on her terms and on her own. But when she finds herself snowed in on Nymph Island with firefighter Josh Carson, her views on what she needs in her life slowly begin to change. But is she ready to relinquish her tight grip on controlling all the details of her life in order to have love? Or will Josh's own secrets push them further apart?

First Oram Productions Edition: March 2016

Cover design by Jean Oram

Dedication

To my grandmothers. For helping me rediscover Muskoka each summer.

A Note on Muskoka

Muskoka is a real place in Ontario, Canada, however, I have taken artistic license with the area. While the issues presented in this book (such as water shed, endangered animals, heritage preservation, shoreline erosion, taxation, etc.) as well as the towns are real, to my knowledge, there is no Baby Horseshoe Island nor is there a Nymph Island, or even a company called Rubicore Developments. The people and businesses are fictional, with the exception of The Kee to Bala and Jenni Walker—you can read about how she ended up visiting Muskoka in the acknowledgements.

Muskoka is a wonderful area where movie stars and other celebrities do vacation. Yet, having spent many summers in the area during my youth and adulthood, I have yet to see a single celebrity—though a man I presume to be Kurt Browning's (a famous Canadian figure skating Olympian) father did offer to help me when the outboard fritzed out on me once. Damn outboard.

You can discover more about Muskoka online at www.discovermuskoka.ca/

Acknowledgments

Thank you to reader Hannah Shows for naming Josh Carson (JC). I hope you enjoy his adventures!

Thank you also goes to the women who help keep me and this story on track: Evelyn, Cali, Margaret, Emily, Erin, and Michelle. Thank you.

And one more big thank you goes to my readers. I couldn't do this journey without you. I hope you have a wonderful, warm holiday season full of all the greatest things in life.

Love and Mistletoe

Aug 2017

To the Sylvan Lake Library,

Jo ice fishing + snowshoeing!

xo

Jean Oram

Chapter One

Simone Pascal fidgeted with her purse, her agitation growing as the meeting went on. She sat back, not joining in as the women built off each other's ideas, ping-ponging them through the group, morphing each one from a kernel into something new and groundbreaking that would give them a competitive edge that always led their businesses to the top.

The Meeting of the Minds women came together every three months to discuss their world domination plans, and had a track record that just about guaranteed someone in their group snagged a million-dollar deal in the fashion industry each quarter.

Simone, despite being at least a decade or two younger than the majority of the members, had already landed at the top of her game, thanks to the group, and she knew who to turn to if she ever needed anything in her designing business or boutique. But what she needed now was something they couldn't provide, and there was only one uncharted frontier left if she was going to have it all. She required help, but not from the MOMs.

She checked the antique watch she'd received from her good friend Melanie Summer.

Five minutes. She couldn't wait any longer.

The watch reminded her of all that was important. Her friends, the Summers, had found exactly what she wanted for herself:

Love. Family. Support. Someone to hold her during the long Canadian winter nights, especially when her world got shaky. She'd incorrectly assumed all those good things would just happen for her, even though her past kept showing her she wasn't good girlfriend material. She was missing whatever it was that made men stay, whatever it was that showed them that what she was doing *was* love.

Simone packed up her ever-present design sketchbook and meeting notes, taking a moment to watch the women who had helped her so much over the years. While she'd never once believed she'd ever hold anything back from this group, she knew they wouldn't understand where she was at and what she needed to do to achieve her next goal. Nobody would—from her father to her friends. But these women surrounding the boardroom table were dynamos that balanced and juggled everything with ease. They just *did* it, and Simone wasn't as lucky. She needed help.

She stood, excusing herself.

"Where are you going?" asked Wanda, a bridal boutique owner from the small town of Blueberry Springs. Her eyes were wide with surprise, and she kept one hand on Simone's chair as though she planned on keeping her in the room no matter what.

"I have a flight."

"You've missed flights before because we've run long," she said, suspicion lacing her words.

Simone felt the prickle of sweat tear up her spine. "I have to do something."

Around the table, eyebrows lifted, waiting for the reveal.

"What could be more important than this?" one of the women asked. Everyone made this group's meetings a priority—that's why it worked. That and the way they checked their egos at the door, held nothing back and ensured things didn't become

Love and Mistletoe

personal. Even here, on Christmas Eve, the women were hashing it out in person on the West Coast at 8:00 a.m., not a single member absent.

Simone's mind stuttered to a stop.

It was 8:00 a.m. Pacific time. That meant it was 11:00 a.m. eastern.

She shoved her chair back, clutching her belongings to her chest. "I'm sorry." Simone knew she was jumpy, sweat clinging to her brow. She was acting like the poster girl for I Have Something to Hide, but she had to go, couldn't explain.

The women watched, mouths hanging open, as Simone exited the room. She rifled through her purse until her hand closed around salvation. Just a few more moments.

She rushed into the bathroom down the hall, her fingers trembling as she latched the stall's lock. She flipped down the toilet seat and plunked herself on top of it, her sketchpad and notes tumbling to the floor in her haste. She adjusted the syringe's plunger over the flesh near her hip, her heart racing with anticipation. She closed her eyes and bit her lip. This was always the worst part.

She sucked in a slow breath. *Don't think. Just do it.*

The needle hovered above her skin and the tiny walls swam, pressing closer.

Do it, Simone.

After inhaling a quick, sharp breath, she jabbed the needle into her flesh, letting out a cry as she shoved the plunger down, then ripped the syringe out as quickly as possible. Relief flowed through her and she let out a shuddery breath. She was good for another twenty-four hours.

She hung her head, collecting herself, before realizing she'd dropped the syringe in her haste. It had rolled under the door and was nestled, spent, between a pair of cherry-red Louboutins.

"Simone?" It was Wanda, her voice demanding, unyielding.

Simone scrambled to collect the syringe, banging her head on the closed stall door, her neck contorting as she fell short of her goal, forced to watch, powerless, as a hand with heavily lacquered nails closed around her secret.

"Open up!" Wanda demanded from the other side of the door. "We need to talk. Now."

Simone eased back onto the toilet seat, not ready for a confrontation with a woman she respected so greatly.

Wanda banged on the stall door with enough force that it sprang open, clanging against the wall. "Explain the meaning of this." The syringe lay on her open palm, the woman towering over her.

More members of MOM poured into the washroom, surrounding Wanda, trapping Simone. They gasped when they saw the needle, one woman having the foresight to ask, "Are you diabetic?"

Simone shook her head and the looks of disappointment ran so deep that she had to turn her gaze away.

"You don't understand," she began, her voice wobbling. "You make it all look so easy and I just want..." Her voice grew thick and she had to swipe at her eyes, not caring if she sent streaks of mascara across her cheeks.

"I do understand, but *this*?" Wanda shook the empty syringe at her.

"I can't...I..."

"We know the pressure can be tough, but it's not worth it. Take a break. You're at the top of your game. Delegate. I'll send you my best virtual assistants. Anything is better than this."

"I know of a good rehab," another woman offered.

"Rehab?" Simone felt the room spin. They thought she was on drugs. That she was shooting up to maintain the energy she needed to get ahead. But she was already at the top of her game—there was nowhere left to go. No more mountains to climb.

All but one and it had nothing to do with fashion or design.

The women closed in. "Simone, don't make excuses," someone murmured.

"Don't deny this," Wanda prompted gently. "We can help."

Tears sprang to Simone's eyes. The MOMs meant the world to her, but this was the one thing they couldn't help her with. Nobody could, and she was running out of time.

"This explains why you were so fidgety in the meeting. You needed a fix!" a fellow member accused.

"No!" Simone scrunched her eyes closed, the room feeling too small, her voice too quiet, too weak. "It's not that."

They all began talking at once, so Simone stood, raising her voice to be heard as she let her secret out of the bag. "They're fertility drugs. I'm trying to have a baby."

All eyes shot to her left hand, checking for a ring.

"Alone."

SIMONE HIGHTAILED IT OUT of the Toronto International Airport and into the blustery December weather badgering the lakeside city. The MOM confrontation hours ago, back on the rainy West Coast, had not been her idea of fun. They, at least, had implicitly understood how difficult it was to find a man who was not only confident enough in his manhood to be with someone who earned oodles more than he did, but also didn't take her level of business commitment personally. That had been enough for them to get behind her having a baby on her own, without having to discuss cysts, ovaries, and operations that would soon leave her barren.

Either way, she was definitely off her game. Not just for revealing her secret, but for messing up the time zones and, as a result, falling three hours behind on her hormone injection schedule. When she'd accidentally forgotten an injection last month it had meant no baby. How was she supposed to be a good mother if she couldn't even keep to a simple once-a-day, make-a-baby commitment? What if she forgot to feed her baby or left it somewhere? She negotiated million-dollar deals with ease and had designs in Milan, London, and New York, and yet couldn't seem to stay on the stupid schedule.

She needed to pull herself together. She couldn't keep messing up and she couldn't wait for Mr. Right, either. She had to do this and she had to do it now, in case the cysts decided to take more than just her ovaries. The doctors had said she could freeze her eggs and use a surrogate, but there was no way a control freak like herself could get behind the idea of entrusting someone else with such an important job as carrying her baby.

"Simone!"

She startled, not expecting to bump into anyone she knew. And that voice brought back a torrent of unwelcome childhood memories that, in her current mood, left her wondering if she should ignore the call and run.

She turned, facing her father, Thomas Pascal.

"Dad, Merry Christmas. I'm sorry, I'm catching a flight to Muskoka and don't have a lot of time."

Behind her dad, her "stepmother," Tricia—who was nearly the same age as Simone—shifted from foot to foot, a tentative smile playing on her lips.

Her father ushered Simone toward his black sedan, parked at the curb. "We'll give you a lift."

"It's okay, I've booked a shuttle."

He opened the rear passenger door and she bristled. If she

wanted to get in, she could open the door herself, but him doing so became unwanted pressure. Simone felt as though he'd already made the decision for her, completely dismissing her thoughts on the matter.

"We'll give you a lift," he repeated.

"What's wrong?" Simone asked. She pressed one hand against the cold metal of the car's roof. Not only was it unusual for her dad to know where she was, but the fact that they had *both* taken the forty-five minute trip to the airport to shuttle her to a charter flight meant something was not right on planet earth. Thomas was not that kind of father. Never had been and never would be.

"We have a little Christmas gift," he said with a grin, nudging her into the sedan, closing the door behind her.

A gift?

The car's heat enveloped her, a welcome change from the bitter weather outdoors, and Simone wondered what the gift could be. She gave a reluctant sigh, then pulled the seat belt across her hips, wincing as it pressed against her sore injection site. She needed to either get over her queasiness with needles so she stopped bruising, or conceive. Preferably the latter. And the sooner, the better.

Her father helped Tricia into the front passenger seat with uncharacteristic care. Was she unwell? What was going on? Simone leaned forward, hoping to catch a hint of what was coming.

Although when she thought about it, her father had always treated his second wife like gold. And even though Tricia and Simone were only a few years apart in age, there had always been an annoying double standard in terms of his treatment and expectations. The woman was quiet, unassuming, and as far as Simone had noted, possessed no desire to succeed or get ahead in the world, making her wonder what her father saw in Tricia. She was Simone's opposite in almost every way when it came to personality, but still managed to bring out Simone's competitive edge every time.

"What's wrong?" she repeated. "How did you know I was here?"

"I was talking to your mother," Thomas said.

Oh, boy. Things were definitely amiss. As far as Simone knew, her parents hadn't spoken in ages. As it was, Simone and her father connected only about three times a year, and almost always she phoned him, on his birthday, Father's Day, or Christmas Day. But never Christmas Eve. And he was here in person.

Not good.

"She has the flu," her father added, checking his blind spot for traffic as he pulled away from the terminal. "She asked that I pass on the word that you shouldn't come over tonight."

Simone felt an uncharacteristic pang of abandonment as well as an irrational flash of anger toward her father. Why was he suddenly involved in their lives? Why hadn't her mother called to tell her? Why did she tell Thomas, of all people? Now, instead of it being two old maids spending the holidays together, Simone was simply alone.

"She said she will likely be feeling better tomorrow afternoon and that you could come over then."

Things were definitely getting weirder, and Simone pulled out her phone to send a text to her mom, hoping her father was mistaken. It wouldn't be the first time.

"You were working today?" he asked.

"A meeting." One she wasn't sure she would have the honor of participating in again.

"Good for you. So many people think they can take the day off just because it has Christmas in its title. People like that will never get ahead." He caught her eye in the rearview mirror. "Mark my words."

"I know," she breathed, predicting the next line of argument, about how she needed to work harder and smarter than everyone else to get to the top. Been there, done that, got the T-shirt and found its style didn't suit her as much as she'd thought it would.

"Are you working tomorrow? There's no reason not to, since you don't attend church." Her father's voice was louder, telling her he'd noticed that she'd tuned him out and that this was his second time asking about her plans.

She sighed, feeling a sudden plunge of exhaustion. "Yes, Dad."

"Good. You can reach further than you have been. Be smart with your time, delegate. What are you working on next?"

Simone hedged. "I'm just wrapping up details from my latest deals." Would it kill him to say, "Good job. I'm proud of you"? She knew she shouldn't care what he thought and that she should have stopped trying to impress him ages ago, but she still heard his voice in her mind, driving her forward as she worked toward her goals, spurring her to get up and tackle the next mountain, to dust herself off when she got knocked down, and zip back in, head down, ready to charge.

It was exhausting.

"So?" he prompted. "What's next?"

"Nothing I can talk about yet." *And nothing you would approve of.*

"You need a plan. You need to be able to see your next five steps."

"I have it under control, Dad."

"Thomas, let her be," Tricia scolded gently, and Simone was surprised she'd spoken up on her behalf. "Simone is doing really well."

"Thanks," she said quickly. Things were getting weirder and

weirder and she was relieved to see her father finally pulling over to drop her off for her next flight. She climbed out, hauling her laptop and overnight bag along behind her. "Thanks for the ride. Have a nice Christmas."

"Simone..." Her father came around the car, hurrying to meet up with her on the sidewalk.

Tricia climbed out, too, smiling, mittened hands clasped in front of her.

"Are you guys okay?" Simone asked, feeling worried. She rarely saw the couple and had no clue what was going on in their lives, only that this was unprecedented and definitely unnerving.

Tricia grinned, her shoulders up around her ears, hands out as though expecting a hug, as Thomas said, "We're expecting a baby."

Chapter Two

Josh Carson stopped midstep in shoveling his neighbor's driveway, contemplating the friend he hadn't seen in well over a month.

"What have you been up to these days?" Dustin repeated.

Josh had begun to hate the question and the awkward dance of elusiveness he inevitably ended up doing to avoid giving himself away. And worse, this time it would be with a fellow smoke jumper. Trust was of the utmost importance between jumpers, as they often held each other's lives in their hands, and now he was going to lie by omitting the one part of his life that finally felt right.

But he knew a man such as Dustin wouldn't understand, and that there would be too much ribbing, too much that Josh wouldn't be able to take without lashing out as he'd done so many times before. But this time, instead of protecting someone else, he'd be protecting himself.

"Staying out of trouble," he replied, leaning against the shovel for a moment as though contemplating whether he had dutifully summed up the past several months of his life. He gave Dustin a cocky grin before continuing on with his job. "Got anyone knocked up yet?"

"None that I know of." His friend chuckled, slapping him on

the back with a gloved hand, his laughter punctuated by clouds of warm air that burst from his lungs.

Josh gave the man a friendly yet unencouraging smile. It was Christmas Eve and he had plans that didn't involve bailing a pal out of trouble.

"What about you? Finally find someone to keep you warm?" Dustin asked.

"Nope."

Women were inherently problematic. They liked to stick the thin edge of their crowbar into his life, hoping to crack him open and spill out the contents as if he were a piñata. No, thank you.

"Nobody?" Dustin asked in disbelief.

Josh, unlike his friend, had become weary of the trouble that usually came with a no-strings-attached good time.

"Did you go gay?"

"No," Josh snapped, struggling to block out memories of men crowding around his father, asking the same pointed question. The disgust in their voices. The taunting. Shoving. Attempts to punish the man for having the courage to show he was different.

There had been more than one occasion where Josh had seen his father's nose bloody, his gut hit so hard he couldn't straighten up to stand tall against the attacks. Josh had learned to fight fast and dirty in order to protect his dad, who had, years later, decided to undergo the transformation from Patrick to the person he had always meant to be—Patricia.

His father's sex change wasn't a secret, but it also wasn't something Josh brought up, particularly in testosterone-fueled gangs such as the smoke-jumping crew. If you were different, you got beat up in life. It was that simple.

"Then why aren't you out chasing tail? We're in our prime, man." Dustin flexed his biceps to illustrate how much firefighting had done for their bodies, the impact lost under layers of winter outerwear. "I need a wingman and the chicks dig you."

"Not interested."

"You all right?" Dustin asked.

"Fine." Josh had returned to clearing the driveway, jerking the shovel harder than he had to in order to send snow flying onto the piles lining the asphalt driveway.

"Oh, right. You're touchy about that whole homosexual thing." Dustin deadpanned with an expressionless face. "Because you're gay."

Josh continued working as though he hadn't heard the ribbing, aware he was probably going to break the shovel's handle if he pushed any harder.

Awkward silence settled over them until, feeling as though he was being judged, Josh said, "Live and let live, man. No need to be a jerk about something that doesn't impact you."

"Is your dick as soft as your heart?"

Josh raised an eyebrow in challenge, unblinking, as the odd snowflake drifted down, the sky continuing to darken, bringing with it a blanket of colder air. The smoke jumpers had dubbed him The Finisher for the way he ended any fight, always coming out on top.

"I'm soft?"

Dustin lost the staring contest by looking away first. "Well, except for that mean left hook of yours."

He continued to glare.

Dustin sighed. "And that swing kick thing you do to knock people down."

Josh tossed a handful of snow at him, showing him that all was forgotten and forgiven.

His friend smirked, ducking. "Easy to see why you're single. Softy."

Josh snorted, thinking how his buddy wasn't that far off base. His latest projects were definitely far from masculine.

He wordlessly pushed his shovel against Dustin's chest, then picked up a wider one from the snowbank by the garage. Together they finished clearing Mrs. Star's driveway before she could come out and fuss like nobody's business.

"Hey, I wanted to ask..." Dustin began as they dumped the borrowed shovels beside Mrs. Star's garage. Immediately, Josh knew his friend had a woman on the line and something was standing in the way of him discovering the color and texture of her lingerie.

"It's Christmas Eve. I have a commitment," Josh replied.

He planned to warm up his half-frozen hands, then drive over to Bracebridge to have a hot chocolate and Bailey's with his half sister Polly as per their ongoing tradition. It had begun around the time the two of them had moved out of their blended-family home and needed to steel themselves before returning there on Christmas Eve. To her father and his mother—biological, not the medically and hormonally enhanced version he used to call Dad—and all the family politics and pressure that went on with that little not-so-fun reunion.

Seeing as Polly's divorce was now under way, he figured she was going to need an extra shot of something warm and fortifying before facing the firing squad of advice from their meddling parents.

"Aw. Come on, man," Dustin begged. "Please?"

That level of whining? Had to be a Scandinavian. "Blonde?"

His friend grinned.

"Blue eyes?"

The grin got wider.

Josh merely shook his head, watching a courier van stop in front of his place. A young woman about their age popped out, her dyed golden locks woven into a high bun similar to a ballerina's. Josh watched his friend out of the corner of his eye. The woman strode toward them with a grace that hinted at flexibility and fitness.

"Hi. I'm looking for a Josh Carson?" She waved a box.

Dustin intercepted Josh. "Working Christmas Eve?"

"I know, right?" She brushed a wisp of hair off her forehead, beaming up at Dustin.

"What could be so special that needs delivering today? Shouldn't a nice woman like you be home with someone doting on you, instead of schlepping through the snow for doofuses like my friend here who can't figure out when to order their gifts so they arrive early?"

She blushed, due to the intensity of Dustin's steady gaze, and Josh elbowed him out of the way to scrawl his signature across the delivery confirmation screen.

"When do you get off?" Dustin was leaning in, pouring on the charm. "I have a lot of time at the moment. I'm a smoke jumper."

Josh could have sworn her knees softened, ready to buckle as she gazed up at his friend. Josh made a swipe for the box, but Dustin tucked it out of reach, not wanting to interrupt the spell he was weaving like a web.

"Isn't Miss Scandinavia waiting for you?" Josh asked loudly.

Dustin gave him a sour look as the spell broke, the courier babe slipping away with a quick "Merry Christmas!"

"Cockblocker," Dustin said, smacking him in the chest with the box as the van spun away.

Josh shrugged, grinning. He clutched the package with both hands, but his pal refused to release it.

"What is this, anyway? A gift for me?" Dustin twisted the box so he could see the Customs declaration form. His face darkened with disappointment as he read the contents.

Time to put up the walls.

Dustin glanced at him in disbelief. "A BeDazzler?"

"It's not for me." Josh wrenched the box free, losing his battle to be cool. "It's Christmas, dickhead."

"What are you up to? You're up to something." His friend was tracking closer, eyes on the prize—Josh's secrets.

"Beer?" Josh tucked his BeDazzler under his arm and opened the front door to his one-story. The welcoming warmth of the entry reminded him how cold it had become outside and how unforgiving Canada's winter could be. They were in for some weather tonight.

"Nah. Maybe next time. I've gotta run." Nevertheless, Dustin stepped inside, throwing an arm around Josh's shoulder in a brotherly way. "Just came by to wish my bachelor friend a merry Christmas." He gave him a big, cheesy grin.

"That's why text messages were invented." Josh gave Dustin's arm a pointed look and his friend awkwardly dropped the embrace.

"Right. So. I was hoping you could do me a small favor."

"I'm committed."

"I'm supposed to get something to Evander de la Fosse—I'm helping out Tyrone Bellingham tonight. You know the guys? Big. Former military. Working on security systems over at the Baby Horseshoe Island development? Ringing any bells?"

Josh nodded. Evander had hooked up with one of Polly's friends, Daphne Summer.

"Tyrone's sister is smoking hot, by the way," Dustin interjected. "Anyway, I told Tyrone I'd get the item to Evander. Tonight."

"And?" Josh asked, ready to push his buddy out the door and close it. Lock it. Move on with his evening. He wasn't in the mood for a wild-goose chase. And anything involving Dustin always ended in some sort of scavenger hunt.

"I kind of double booked myself. There's this hot woman..." He shaped an hourglass in the air with his hands. "Fireplace, red wine... You know how it is."

"I have plans."

"Hey, didn't your sister get divorced?"

"She's off-limits."

"I'll let you jump out of the plane first next season if you let me comfort her."

Josh had spent two years fighting house fires, then moved on to the ego's equivalent of leveling up—smoke jumping. While he didn't mind the way women looked at him when he told them what he did for a living, the job was starting to mess with his head, and a part of him doubted he'd be there to jump next spring. Lately, he'd been overreacting to anything fire related and had installed extra smoke detectors in his home—above and beyond code. He'd even found himself testing the devices in his friends' homes, as well as checking fire escapes on taller buildings. It was becoming a problem. An embarrassing one he suspected would go away if he found something else to do for a living.

With the box still balanced under his arm, he shoved Dustin out the door. "Good night. Merry Christmas. Good luck."

His friend, a desperate gleam in his eyes, shoved his foot in the doorjamb. "She's Swedish."

Josh laughed.

"She leaves the country the day after tomorrow."

Josh laughed harder. Dustin's problems were so minor.

"Five hundred bucks."

Josh stopped laughing. "You're serious about this one?"

"A grand. Please?"

Wow. Dustin was actually begging. And Josh could use the money. Another reason he hadn't left smoke jumping yet. A guy like him didn't have a ton of options in this economy. Plus it didn't help that he was well-suited for smoke jumping. Even as a kid, he'd always had escape plans at the ready. How to get away if things got bad. Always made sure he had at least two exits, as well as a backup plan. Which made him great at his job, sticking another gold star on his damn ego.

"A grand?" he confirmed. His friend had to be joking. But a thousand bucks would buy a lot of supplies and could be worth any wild-goose chase.

No. He couldn't do that to Polly. Not tonight. He'd made a promise and she was way more important than Dustin's flavor of the week.

"She needs my help, Josh."

"What do you mean?" He was aware his voice had taken on a hard edge. "Is she in trouble?"

"I need to show her that not all men are bad."

"Meaning what?" He moved closer, his senses sharpening.

"Her last boyfriend was a little abusive."

"A little?" The cardboard box with the BeDazzler bent under Josh's arm.

"Emotionally."

"Emotionally?"

"He called her fat."

"Forget it." Josh tossed the dented box onto a pile of shoes by the door. He should have known better than to listen to Dustin unless they were in the midst of a forest fire—then the man was always dead-on.

"Please?" he begged again.

"No."

"Come on. She was really upset. I promise I won't track Polly—ever."

Josh gave him a sharp look.

"Please? Super-easy job." Dustin placed his hands under his chin, looking pathetic as he attempted puppy-dog eyes. "It won't take long. The delivery is even in your direction—Bracebridge."

"Promise?"

"Promise."

Josh sighed, softening. "Fine. Whatever." He could drop it off on the way to Polly's and collect an easy grand, if that was all it took. "But you owe me. Big. As in *really* big." He shook his head and put out his hand, expecting a package or instructions. "What do I have to do?"

Dustin passed him a padded envelope from inside his down jacket. "Give Evander de la Fosse, the bodyguard, this. Tonight." He laid a hand over the envelope, giving each word special emphasis. "Has to be tonight. Life or death."

JOSH HAD SPENT THE PAST forty-five minutes trying to track down Evander and was starting to think the delivery was less about life-or-death and more of a wild-goose chase intended to free up Polly so Dustin could comfort her.

Although if Dustin was telling the truth and it wasn't about Polly, how much was *he* getting for the delivery if he was planning to reward Josh with a cool grand? Either way, the package had to be pretty important. Josh gently pressed his fingers into the padded envelope, thinking. Some sort of spy device, or evidence needed to crack a case? It didn't seem likely, and while the package was light enough to be considered empty, it had a small pebble-like bump, proving it wasn't. He shook the thing. Nothing. He held it to his nose and inhaled. Smelled like a plastic-padded envelope.

Josh dialed his sister, wanting to remove the sneaking suspicion that he was holding a packaged piece of trash so his buddy would be free to bed Polly while her protective stepbrother was busy. And while the idea might seem extreme, he knew Dustin had a thing for women who were on the rebound, and his sister definitely qualified as she waited for her ex to adhere to their prenup. Polly deserved more than a meaningless one-night stand, which was all Dustin ever offered.

"Polls?" he said when she answered.

"Are you coming over or what?"

"I'm on my way. I just have to do one thing. Is Dustin there?"

"No, why should he be? Is he running from his latest woman's old man and his shotgun?" She sounded amused. Which meant she'd had two drinks at least. Two more and she'd be looking for a place to nap. He'd better plan on being the driver once he unloaded the dang package. "How long will you be, anyway? I've already had five texts from your mom."

"Only five? We've got a few hours before she blows her lid, then." Josh paused for a second, tapping the envelope against his thigh. Polly knew Hailey. Hailey was Daphne Summer's sister. Daphne was living with Evander.

Josh may have just found the lead he needed to complete his task.

Phone to his ear, he began hurrying to his truck, the snowflakes drifting down around him growing more grainy than they had been half an hour ago. "Polls? Where's Evander de la Fosse tonight?"

"Evander? With Daphne. Why?"

"Because he's not at home and I need to see him."

"So?"

Josh summoned patience. He could tell from Polly's tone that she was holding back, playing the straight card. In other words, messing with him.

"Where's Daphne?" he asked sweetly.

"With her sisters," she replied just as sweetly.

Despite his focus on getting the package off his hands ASAP, he found himself chuckling. He needed a woman in his life who could dish things back at him like Polly, yet was understanding at the same time. Without the icky, annoying sister part, of course.

Why was he dreaming, anyway? He had a life to get in order, and after that only a certain type of woman would be interested in him. And he was certain she'd be nearly impossible to find.

He sighed and pushed a hand through his hair, dislodging snowflakes. "And where are Daphne's sisters?" he asked, starting his vehicle.

"At their cottage."

"And where is—"

"You have to go to Nymph Island?" Polly complained. "That'll take *forever*. No, wait. The lake probably isn't even all the way frozen yet. Ha, ha. You have to stay on land and drink with me."

"Then how did they get there?"

"Helicopters."

Damn billionaires.

"I'm putting on the kettle for a hot chocolate and Bailey's right now."

He let out a laugh at her assumed victory. "I made a promise, Polls. I've got to see this through." He heard grumbling on the other end of the line. "Just an hour. Promise."

"You and your damn promises. How are you even going to get there?"

That was going to be the trick, wasn't it? He ended the call, pulling out onto the street.

Forty-five minutes later he found himself crossing a frozen Lake Rosseau on his snowmobile, the local fishermen having assured him that it was indeed his lucky day, as the lake had frozen over early this year, making it safe to sled on.

Josh was going to have to make sure he got Polly a little something extra for her stocking tomorrow morning, because at this rate he wasn't making it back to her place within the hour he'd promised. And while it was only ten kilometers across the lake to Nymph Island and ten back, he had to take it slow in case there were unexpected areas of thin ice or open water.

After slowing to check his GPS, Josh glanced up at the nothingness above him. Earlier in the day the clouds had been gray and low, the temperature dropping, and now with the night fully upon him the chill had intensified, the world had turned eerie and dark.

Back on track, Josh hugged the shore of an island, where he knew the ice would be thicker, enjoying the way fresh drifts puffed up around him like icy confetti. There were worse ways to spend Christmas Eve than riding across the lake. Maybe he'd even go in for a warm drink if those cute Summer sisters were feeling welcoming.

He rounded a small horseshoe-shaped island and spotted his goal, marked by a flicker of light high in the trees. He parked his machine beside the Nymph Island dock, not wanting to drive up the path in case his sled hit something under the snow or he tore up the landscaping. The silence felt almost deafening, but he left his helmet on, knowing that his body heat would escape quickly if he removed it. He flipped up his visor, finding the scent of fresh snow crisp, clean and invigoratingly nippy. On second thought, he might have to skip staying for a drink, as a cold front was definitely coming in. If the weather kept up there'd be whiteout conditions within an hour or two and then it wouldn't matter how good he was, because if he couldn't see squat, including his GPS, he could consider himself royally pooched.

Bundled in his helmet and snowmobile suit, Josh followed a trail of footprints up the hill. The only sound breaking the silence of the night was a generator that powered the island, giving the rustic old cottage a homey glow as light poured from its windows.

He trudged up the incline, snow crunching underfoot. He made his way onto the steps that led up to the old cottage's wraparound veranda. Someone had recently cleared the way, although the odd icy bit had been left behind. As he climbed the stairs he could see through the large porch windows. Four couples cozily enjoying themselves came into view, leaning against each other as they laughed. They were warmed by the flames roaring in the fireplace, a beautifully sad lone woman sitting on the outskirts of the group.

He felt like an intruder. An outsider. Someone who didn't belong here.

He almost turned away, afraid to break up the scene. His foot fell through the third step from the top, and he caught himself with a muffled thump that drew all eyes to him. A large man placed himself in front of a petite woman and a little girl in a party dress. With surprising speed for a guy his size, he ate up the space between himself and the French doors. Josh whipped off his helmet so Evander would recognize him, then doubted the move. The headgear might offer protection, since the bodyguard obviously hadn't figured out who he was, and came roaring through the door.

Josh fumbled for the envelope in his snowsuit's inside breast pocket as the man leaped across the veranda, taking him down before he had a chance to speak. As Josh fell backward, he watched the envelope spin through the air above them. Then the impact of their tumble down the stairs jolting through him and he lost his wind, the big, bulky man squeezing his lungs dry like a sponge until darkness shut him out.

Chapter Three

Simone had jumped at the invitation to join the Summers and their men out at their cottage on Nymph Island for an impromptu winter picnic, instead of spending Christmas Eve alone, brooding about the fact that her father and stepmother were going to have a baby. Now she pushed the gawking sisters aside and skittered down the icy steps toward the unconscious form lying under a sheepish, protective bear of a man.

"Evander, get off him," she said, pushing at his large shoulder.

Evander slowly complied, keeping his body as a barrier between her and the limp intruder. Sweet.

But also very annoying. It made her want to rail against his protective actions and prove that she could handle herself, thank you very much.

"Careful, he's armed," Evander said as she went to move around him.

Simone froze in her tracks. The unconscious man, blond hair askew over his forehead, didn't seem like the type to carry a weapon or do evil deeds. He seemed...harmless. And completely unprotected. On top of being unconscious.

Evander cautiously patted down the man, checking for weapons. "He was reaching inside his snowsuit."

Daphne handed him an envelope with a wry frown. "He was armed with a message." She tucked a chunk of unruly curls behind an ear and Simone noted that her face looked rounder, more tired than usual. She'd bet Daphne's hunky man had been keeping her up too late, expressing his love and wearing her out.

Simone had tried dating a former military type like Evander once and it most definitely had not worked out, the man finding her inability to accept his help insulting. What she really needed was a guy with enough confidence to be the yin to her yang as needed—to be soft, caring, and understanding. Unfortunately, she had yet to find that in a straight man.

"Don't shoot the messenger," quipped Maya, the second eldest Summer sister, from her perch at the top of the staircase.

Simone watched Evander slowly bring himself down a notch. His training in the military had served him well as a bodyguard for Daphne and her daughter, Tigger, earlier that year, but at the moment his over-the-top reaction left Simone feeling unnerved.

She understood why Evander was still acting protective—he obviously loved Daphne and thought of Tigger as his own, and with the silence that had settled after the whole blowup last summer, he was likely waiting for some sort of surprise counterattack. But this wasn't the navy or secret intelligence. It was Daphne dealing with the father of her five-year-old. While her ex was a big, spoiled, confused jerk, Simone didn't think there was going to be any more trouble. And as opposite as Daphne and Evander seemed to be, they connected on a level Simone hadn't quite figured out yet. But whatever it was, it was good and she didn't want to see it end by him overreacting and trying Daphne's patience.

"Come on, let's get him inside," Simone said, nudging Evander, who immediately stooped to lift the man slowly being covered by gently falling snow.

"Maybe we shouldn't move him," Daphne said, worry lining her brow.

The man in question groaned, his eyes not opening, as he gave a feeble attempt to shift position.

"No spinal damage. He can move. Get him inside," Simone commanded. "Come on, chop, chop. Maya, hold the door. Connor, help out Evander." She stepped aside, hugging herself as Maya's husband came forward. There was moisture in the air that hadn't been there earlier and it was cutting through her fitted sweater like miniature blades of ice.

"It's Josh Carson," Hailey, the eldest Summer sister, said in surprise as the inert man was carried past her.

"JC? Polly's half brother?" Simone hurried up the step to take a better look at their friend's sibling. They'd all gone to the same high school—the Summers, Simone, Polly, and JC—and Simone remembered JC as a fighter she'd wisely steered clear of. Some sort of issues at home, if she recalled. While handsome and a bit of a player, he'd had a quickness that had shifted from sunshine and roses to a fierce fighting stance at the drop of a hat. She'd never figured him out, and luckily, their paths hadn't crossed very often.

"Hasn't he been away fighting forest fires?" Maya asked.

"Smoke jumping," Hailey stated.

Simone shivered, walking alongside, taking in JC's good looks. He was still as cute as all get-out. She'd give him that. Handsome.

Dangerously so.

"Didn't he go to jail or something?" she asked. There had to be a reason this man was bad for her.

"That was Lix Levenson. Failure to appear," Melanie said, straightening as she closed the door behind the group. "They used to run in the same crowd."

"Didn't you date Lix?"

"Unfortunately, yes." Melanie's mouth formed a tight line. Her fiancé, Tristen Bell, gave her a one-armed hug in support, his teenaged daughter, Dot, rolling her eyes at the display of affection.

Lix's story was slowly coming back to Simone. The jerk was the one who had started the whole insecurity thing Melanie had going on with her Marilyn Monroe-esque body. A few comments at the wrong time and her friend was still reeling all these years later. However, thanks to an inadvertent combo move of Simone plying Melanie with homemade 1950s style dresses and her fiancé noticing how sexy they looked on her, she had definitely come into her own. Add in the fact that Tristen had helped her open her own legal aid office and the woman was on top of the world.

The men laid JC on the old orange couch near the fire, then stood back and stared at him. Five-year-old Tigger, who had been silent through it all, brought JC's snowmobile helmet and laid it on his chest, her expression remorseful.

"Evander killed the bad man." She looked up at her mother with large, round eyes, her bottom lip trembling.

"No!" Daphne collapsed onto her knees, hugging her daughter tightly. "He's not dead. Evander just knocked him over, but he's a friend, honey. Evander was just being...careful." She gave her boyfriend a look, but he stood as still as a mountain, hands loose at his sides.

"I'm sorry," he mumbled.

"He's not like Grandma Summer?" Tigger asked, placing her hands on either side of Daphne's face and staring at her.

The room grew hushed at the mention of the recently departed Catherine.

"No, honey," Simone said, reaching down to squeeze Daphne's shoulder as the sisters all fought against tears, their grief still raw and whole. Maya busied herself straightening magazines on the nearby card table, forcibly clearing her throat. "JC's going to be okay," Simone added. "He's just resting after bonking his head."

The figure on the couch moaned again as if to prove his vitality and Tigger squealed and hid behind Evander. He reached behind him to scoop the little girl into his arms, then carried her away from the group, mumbling soothing words. Simone saw tears brim in Daphne's eyes again, but this time out of love instead of grief.

Simone wanted that. Big time.

But she was too self-reliant, too strident. She may as well live with brick walls around herself for all the luck she'd had in the dating world. Thank goodness for modern medicine. She could have a baby with donor 8753 and live happily ever after—without some man harping at her about her inability to show him some love. She could love just fine, thank you. Men just couldn't recognize it because she didn't swoon.

She sighed, then, realizing she was wallowing in self-pity, cleared her throat. "Well?"

"Should we call 911?" Melanie asked.

"Why?" Daphne, still hazy with grief, looked up.

"He's unconscious," Melanie replied drily.

Hailey's husband, Finian Alexander, an A-list movie star, wrapped his arms tighter around his pregnant wife.

They all stared at JC for a long moment, then Simone headed to the kitchen. It was cooler in that part of the cottage, as the kitchen had been added on decades ago and barely benefited from the warmth flowing from the fireplace, the cottage's only heat source. With the pump turned off until spring so the pipes didn't freeze, Simone dug through one of the coolers they'd brought for a bottle of water. She uncapped it, taking a swig to ensure it was nice and brisk.

Perfectly refreshing.

She rejoined the crowd gathered around Josh and, without pausing to take in the way his five o'clock shadow looked devastating against his pale skin, dumped the contents of the bottle on the man's face.

He jolted and sputtered, his hand swiping over his strong jaw in response. His helmet rolled off his chest, hitting the area rug with a thud. He started to sit up, but grew pale and eased back, wincing.

"Simone!" Hailey whispered harshly, giving her a glare before stalking to the kitchen, her maternity jeans slipping lower in her haste. She gave them an impatient tug, quickly returning with a tea towel.

Simone shrugged. He was conscious now. Problem solved, right?

"What happened?" JC asked. His voice was groggy, as though he'd been sleeping for days, and the roughness in it sent ribbons of pleasure down Simone's spine. She quickly banished them. It was just the hormones talking. Which meant they were working. Which meant she'd be pregnant soon and holding a baby by next Christmas. But not with JC. Nope. No way.

Why would she even think that? Of course she wouldn't be here with him. She was having a baby with donor 7658. Or was it 8753? 7857?

Maybe if she could look away from the drops of water clinging to JC's stubble she'd be able to remember. While his hair was light, his facial hair was darker, like an untold secret not everyone knew. The darkness brought out the paleness of his blue eyes, giving his handsomeness an unexpected edge that revved Simone's engine.

"Evander thought you were armed," Daphne said gently, taking the towel from Hailey and dabbing at the water on JC's chin. Simone found herself moving closer, resisting the urge to elbow her friend out of the way so she could take over the gentle ministrations. But instead of allowing Daphne to help, JC took the towel, swiping it along the back of his neck where the water was trailing into his snowsuit.

"You should get out of that," Simone said, her voice cracking. She coughed to clear her throat. "Let it dry." She shrugged when his eyes met hers, and glanced toward the windows, to see the snow still coming down, sticking to the glass. Going out with a wet base layer wasn't smart. Even she knew that. She crossed her arms so she wouldn't be tempted to help him strip.

Daphne passed JC the envelope that had been knocked from his grip during Evander's tackle. "This is yours. I'm Daphne. Daphne Summer. I think you know my sisters." She made a quick round of introductions, starting with her sisters, their men, and then Tigger and Dot before completing the circle with Simone.

Her and JC's eyes locked and she had to glance away, not trusting herself not to stare, not to reveal her longing. She'd dated men like him before and it had always ended with the guy dumping her, leaving her with a broken heart, because under all the macho bravado he didn't have what it took to be with a woman who was strong and independent.

JC waved the envelope, leaning forward to brace himself with an elbow on his knee. "It's for Evander." He tentatively probed the back of his head.

Simone had a perfect view of JC's broad shoulders and the way his torso tapered down to his waist, evident even under the bulky snowsuit. Her need to memorize his every detail made her feel as though she'd never seen a man before, and she forced herself to look away once again.

"What is it?" Daphne asked, turning the envelope over in her hands before handing it to Evander, who snatched it, quickly tucking it in the back of his jeans.

"What do I owe you for delivery?"

"Say thank you!" Daphne scolded, arms crossed.

"Thank you," the bodyguard muttered.

"It's already covered," JC said, sending more shivers trickling down Simone's spine. He needed coffee so he'd wake up and lose that bedroom quality to his voice. What were the chances there was still some left here from the summer?

"What is it?" Daphne asked again.

Tigger's eyes lit up. "Is it a super bright fairy light to help me sleep at night? You promised you'd get me one and it's almost Christmas. Can I open it? Can I?" She began bouncing, snagging Evander's arm. "Mom, you said I could open one present tonight and I choose that!"

"It's not big enough to be a super bright fairy light," JC mumbled. "The wings would break off."

"Maybe it unfolds and pops up when you take it out of the package," Tigger replied.

"You know what a super bright fairy light is?" Simone asked Josh, suspicion edging into her mind. If she had no clue what it was, how did a big tough guy like him know? Did he have kids?

Of course he had kids. Practically everyone their age did.

Except her. But she was getting there, wasn't she?

"Let's have supper before we worry about any gifts, okay?" Daphne cast Evander a curious look before heading to the kitchen with Hailey and Maya to set out the picnic supper.

The bodyguard pulled on a down jacket and excused himself to go to the outhouse, where Simone suspected he'd check out the contents of the mystery envelope in privacy.

"What's in it?" she asked JC as soon as he'd gone.

The man merely shrugged. He attempted to stand, saying his sister was waiting, but his legs gave up on the task, sending him reeling into Simone, who caught him and plunked him back on the couch. Holding him, even through his thick, padded outerwear, felt too close, too intimate, too tempting and therefore dangerous.

"I dunno," she said skeptically as she blocked him from trying to stand again. "You don't really seem up to it and I think Polly would rather you wait a few minutes before going out across the lake. Alone."

"Totally," Tristen's daughter agreed. Her streak of green hair fell into her eyes and she flicked it out of the way. She'd been quietly sitting at the edge of the room, watching, and Simone had almost forgotten about her.

"Do you have a bump?" Simone asked, holding herself back from checking his skull.

"Yeah," JC said, his fingers diving into his hair to check.

"We need to ice it," Melanie murmured. She zipped into the kitchen for a plastic bag, then filled it with snow off the veranda.

"You shouldn't drive," Dot said.

Simone nodded. "We can give you a ride back later."

"I need to get my sled home. I promised my mom a ride tomorrow."

"Then we'll get it tomorrow," Simone said, taking the cold pack from Melanie and awkwardly offering it to JC. She almost caved in to the desire to apply it herself, to sit close and nurse him back to health, maybe even allow herself to brush up against his muscled arm.

Which, once again, told her the hormones were working.

"I'll have the helicopter come get you," Connor MacKenzie said, pulling out his cell phone. The man had once been nicknamed the King of Toronto and was now starting a whole new business venture with his bride, Maya. Lately it seemed as though the two of them were closing million-dollar deals each month. They were impatient types, having eloped only weeks after they met. However, it was definitely working for them so far.

They were already ahead of the game by decades. "You should have a doctor take a look at that bump."

"Is it bleeding?" Dot asked, her voice filled with both awe and disgust.

JC shook his head.

"Do you remember what happened?" Simone asked, sitting beside him. His pupils appeared to be the same size, but that didn't rule out a concussion. You didn't lose consciousness for nothing.

JC thought for a moment, then said, "I remember walking up the path and seeing everyone in the cottage, and then waking up inside it."

Simone shared a look with Finian, who drew in a long breath. He turned to Connor. "Got any cell coverage?"

The other man shook his head, adjusting the neck on his tan, cable-knit sweater. Finian checked his own phone before pocketing it again.

"I thought there was a cell signal booster here?" Simone said, a sliver of panic shifting to the forefront of her mind. While she found it relaxing being on the island, as she never seemed to feel the need to compulsively check her email, she didn't like the idea of being entirely cut off from the outside world. She had a lot of skills, but winter survival in the middle of nowhere wasn't one of them.

"That was over on Baby Horseshoe," Finian replied.

Right. And when Finian, Connor, Tristen, and Evander had banded together to buy the island from Daphne's ex and the developer Rubicore, the previous owners had taken everything that wasn't tied down before they turned over the keys.

"I bought one for here," Connor said, "but I lent it to a friend for his hunting cabin and haven't got it back yet." He gave an apologetic frown.

The group grew silent, the only sounds the crackling of burning logs and Hailey, Daphne, and Maya laughing in the kitchen as they prepared supper.

"I'll head up the hill and see if I can get enough signal to call a helicopter in for you," Connor said to JC.

The injured man stood. "I'm fine. A helicopter isn't necessary."

"You bothered by helicopters?" Connor asked, sizing him up.

Simone watched the two position themselves. Cockfights. She hated them. Alphas seemed to get their noses out of joint for the silliest reasons.

"I'm fine with them even when I'm jumping out of one and into a forest fire," JC replied. "I just don't want to put you and your pilot out in a storm on Christmas Eve for a small bump on the head." As if to illustrate how minor it was, JC tossed the bag of ice on the nearby coffee table and tugged the zipper of his suit up to his chin. "Thanks, but I'm heading out. Merry Christmas."

Finian headed him off. "Let's eat first. Give you a minute to clear your head. That was quite a fall."

Connor grabbed his parka off a coat rack and headed for the door as Evander came in, brushing large drifts of snow off his shoulders, his cheeks rosy.

"Bad weather coming in," JC said, eyeing Evander as he moved closer to the door. "Thank you for the invitation, but I'd better make a move while I still can."

"I doubt anyone is going anywhere soon," Evander said, his voice low and commanding. "I just about got lost returning from the outhouse. There's not much in the way of visibility."

"What? It was fine five minutes ago!" Simone protested, moving to the window. The idea of not being able to make a run to the outhouse caused the several cups of coffee she'd drunk on her flight home to slosh inside her. Talk about timing.

"Go in pairs if you're heading up the hill in the dark," Melanie said, entering the room with her sisters. "Supper's ready."

"Nobody's going anywhere," Evander declared.

Josh winced as he put on his helmet. "I have a GPS. I'll be fine if I move fast."

"Could you see the cottage lights from the outhouse?" Connor asked the bodyguard, one eye on JC, who was buckling his chin strap.

"Once I was close, but there's no way you could see them from up the hill. Or from down by the boathouse, for that matter. Not through what's almost a total whiteout." He gave JC a pointed look, knowing the man had left his snowmobile down there.

"We could use rope to guide us up the hill so we don't get lost," Finian said. "In my film *Man versus War*—"

Hailey gave him a playful squeeze. "Okay, Mr. Movie Star. No need for cinema references."

"Yeah? And who had my poster above her bed as a teen?" he teased.

Hailey blushed, pinching him. "Watch it or I'll photograph you in a compromising position."

"I like the sound of that." He carefully scooped the pregnant woman into his arms. "At least we don't have to worry about paparazzi if we're snowed in."

Simone noticed how JC caught the cuddles out of the corner of his eye as he surveyed the weather from the French doors. An expression crossed his face that she didn't quite understand. Was it envy or discomfort?

"Will the helicopter be able to fly in this?" she asked. It didn't sound safe for JC to go zipping off across the lake in this weather, nor for him to ride in a helicopter—an aircraft they couldn't even call in.

He opened the door and a gust of wind blanketed him in snow. He closed it again and looked back at the group.

"Come on, let's make ourselves useful and look for rope," Finian said to Connor, Evander, and Tristen.

"The bin in here has extra boat lines, it might have rope," Melanie said, leading them into a bedroom off the living room.

JC, his hand still on the door, watched the snow come down for a moment before reaching over to tap the single-paned window. "We should close the shutters. We're losing a lot of heat." He headed outside and quickly started latching the wooden panels over the windows.

"Are we stuck?" Simone asked when he returned, stomping the snow off his boots.

"Overnight would be my guess." He tugged the curtains over the French doors.

"Overnight," she echoed, wrapping her arms around herself. Snowed in on Christmas Eve without her morning dose of hormones?

Not on her life.

There had to be a way out of here before then.

"I'm sure it's just a cloud giving us little dose of powder for a perfect white Christmas. That's all." She stood straighter. Mother Nature wasn't going to mess with her plans. She couldn't. They were women. Women had to stick together. It was a rule of sisterhood.

JC turned, tripping on a small area rug with his large winter boots. He swayed like a leaf in an autumn wind as he fought for balance. Simone wrapped her arms around his waist, supporting him. He smelled of snow and snowmobile exhaust. And something else she couldn't put her finger on, but wanted to continue inhaling. Forever.

JC tried to sit on a nearby chair, taking Simone with him. He apologized as she scrambled off him, his hands brushing her breast as he tried to help steady her.

Electricity and need zinged through her and she stood, cheeks heated. This man... This man was way too tempting, especially in the state she was in. She wanted to sit in his lap and kiss those wonderful lips of his, feel the scrub of his five o'clock shadow on her cheeks. Wanted to hear his body sing along with hers.

She fanned her face. "It's warm."

His steady gaze watched her. "Right." He slowly unzipped his snowsuit and Simone had to look away, certain he was teasing her, that he knew the impact his body was having on hers.

She cleared her throat and glanced around the room. It was empty. Everyone had left to go fill their plates or find rope, leaving her with JC as though he was her personal gift from Santa.

She glanced back at the man, who gave her a lopsided, amused grin.

Honestly, she'd rather have a lump of coal.

SIMONE WATCHED EVERYONE break into couples to enjoy their picnic supper in the spacious, open living room, Dot and Tigger laying out a blanket for their own meal. The men hadn't found enough rope to try and make their way up the hill to see if they could wrangle service out of their phones, but Simone was fairly certain the storm would blow over soon. It had to.

In the meantime, the living room had plenty of seating. The only person sitting alone was JC, and after looking around at all the lovebirds, Simone reluctantly settled in the armchair beside him, facing the large fireplace. Even though JC was the kind of man she avoided, sometimes, when you were unlucky in love, sitting with lovebirds hurt.

"How's the head?" she asked. He hadn't thrown up and didn't seem confused, which she took to be good signs. He'd removed his snowsuit and she had to work to train her attention away from the span of his broad shoulders. Whenever she wasn't focused on something such as the wooden snowshoes above the mantel she found herself taking in his pure manliness like a woman who'd been deprived of— Nope, she was not heading off in that forbidden direction again. This was JC. He was a big macho jock type who liked thought-free bimbos. He was the exact opposite of what she was looking for and vice versa. Not that either of them were looking for something that sizzled between the sheets, anyway.

Brain?

Yes.

Shut up now.

"Bit of a headache," JC replied.

"Stick your head in the snow. That should help," Maya suggested from her spot across the room, where she was tapping away on her laptop.

That's what Simone was going to need if she kept thinking—a snow bath to cool her jets.

"Helpful and oh so kind," Hailey quipped.

Simone nodded in automatic agreement, even though she believed JC had no right to look so tempting, and should be punished for it—preferably by something cold and unpleasant.

"She's not the most nurturing of the group," Hailey added, giving her sister a glare.

"What?" Maya said. "It was a good suggestion. Cold will reduce the swelling, which will help decrease the pain."

"I've got something for that," Simone said. She pulled her purse out from under the couch near the armchair she was occupying. She'd almost brought tomorrow's hormone dose with her, just in case, but had been worried one of the sisters would see it in her purse and ask questions she wasn't quite ready to answer. But now she was more worried about the possibility of missing the shot entirely and wasting another month by falling off the schedule again.

She couldn't explain why, but she was afraid to tell the Summer sisters she was going it alone on the baby front. Maybe it was because she'd waited too long to broach the topic and was now in so deep they'd feel hurt by being excluded from something so big. She'd wanted to confide in them when she'd found out about her ovaries in early October, but it had felt so minor compared to the loss of their mother. So she'd waited. But then there had been Hailey's pregnancy announcement, Maya's elopement and Melanie's wedding plans... It had felt as though Simone's petty sorrows and stubbornness in wanting to carry her own child would simply be seen as her being selfish, wanting her own way and trying to get attention or pity instead of sharing in the joys of their lives.

And honestly, it wasn't a big deal to be trying this avenue. Couples did it all the time without announcing it to the world. Besides, she wasn't even sure it would work—it hadn't last month, so why make a big fuss out of what might possibly turn out a dead end?

But if it did work...

Two months. There would be only two months age difference between her half sibling and her child. They would share the same milestones, and anyone who could perform elementary math would realize that Simone had gotten herself knocked up right around the time her father made his big announcement. It would look as though Simone was in a desperate bid against her stepmother for her dad's attention, even though she'd just spent three months adjusting her life priorities, consulting, researching, and going to doctors and fertility clinics. She'd undergone a multitude of invasive tests, filtered through donors, and was weeks into preparing herself, as well as dealing with side effects, but what would it matter in the end? They were going to have a baby first.

Simone handed JC the bottle of acetaminophen, thinking she might have to pop one, too, if the pressure in her head continued to intensify.

"Thanks." He shook out two and handed back the bottle, then flinched when the logs in the fireplace shifted, sending off sparks and causing him to drop the pills onto the area rug. He muttered something about needing to get out of the business, and retrieved the tablets from the floor.

Simone, not wanting to know the meaning of his mumblings, began tucking into her plate of pasta salad and fried chicken, stretching her feet toward the fire. "You have kids?" she asked him, still curious about the fairy light conversation.

"Nope."

She shouldn't feel gleeful hearing that, should she?

"Married?"

"Nope."

Thank you, God.

"You proposing?" he asked with a wicked grin.

She let out a snort, giving him attitude, her body tightening at the casual way he glanced at her. She didn't even know what it was, but it annoyed her how quickly he could get her mind and body off track. She wanted to lick his biceps, which was utterly ridiculous, seeing as he was wearing a long-sleeved, thin sweater. She'd get lint all over her tongue. Plus freak him out and make things awkward.

"It's called making conversation, you Neanderthal. Not all women who see you want to hook you."

His expression turned to one of surprise. She gave him a smug smile, happy to have knocked the panty-dropping grin off his face for the time being. She leaned back in her chair. Even though it was possible she could end up stuck overnight in a place with no running water and heat that barely spread beyond the living room, it could be kind of fun if she got to push JC off his little "I'm so hot" pedestal. Her new life was all about slowing down and having fun again, so why not start now? She was ready to stop worrying about other businesses getting ahead of hers and ready to dropkick pressure out of her life. Ready to find her joy.

She moved her feet as Daphne glided by, placing a juice box on the mantel while she reprimanded her daughter for drinking two in a row.

"Sorry," Dot said. "I thought that was still her first one."

"Tigger, you know all that juice will make you bouncy." Daphne added, "It's okay, Dot. She's a little trickster." She gave her daughter a pointed look, which was returned with a giggle before the five-year-old skipped over to JC, clinging to the arm of his chair as she jumped in place.

"Did you know Nymph Island has fairies?"

JC, who had been about to take a bite of his chicken, paused thoughtfully. "You don't say?"

"I do say!" Tigger placed her elbows on the armrest, leaning close to the man, eyes wide. "They're real!"

"Real?"

Simone watched the exchange, curious as to why JC was taking Tigger so seriously. Was he afraid Evander would knock him out again if he didn't entertain his little girl? If JC wasn't careful he might become one of her new favorites, and she already had four doting men to choose from. Uncle Finian had won her over with a new party dress and tales from Hollywood; Uncle Connor had saved her from a falling tree. Evander had captured her heart with his love, while quiet Uncle Tristen had done so with his gentle ways, big shaggy dog and teenaged daughter.

"Hey, where's your dog, Tristen?" Simone asked.

"At home. Probably crossing his legs," he answered, his face tightening with worry at the thought of his Bernese mountain dog being locked inside for the night.

"I made them fairies houses and they ate the blueberries I left for them," Tigger whispered loudly, still hanging off JC's chair.

"Really?" He leaned closer, as though their conversation was the most interesting thing in the room. Which it kind of was. It had Simone intrigued, mostly due to the way JC seemed so genuine and unexpectedly gentle with Tigger.

"They like shiny things," the girl continued.

"Like sequins?"

"Sequins?" Simone exclaimed. Okay, stop the bus. How did a man like JC know what they were? Shouldn't he be suggesting manly objects such as ball bearings?

He set her back with a look that said, *"We weren't talking to you, lady."*

Well, she knew where she wasn't welcome. The jerk. She'd known his nice side was just a front for a nasty under layer. She took her plate and went to join Hailey at the card table near the stairs that led up to the loft.

"Ugh, I can't stand the smell of chicken," Hailey complained.

"What's wrong with it?" Simone asked, waving her drumstick under her nose. It smelled divine.

"It's just a pregnancy thing." Her friend leaned away, trying not to inhale.

"Oh. Sorry." Simone slouched in the hard-backed chair, then picked up her plate and moved to sit with Daphne, who was watching her daughter, likely worried that she was abusing JC's kindness.

"And other stuff like nickels," Tigger was saying.

"Those would make perfect stepping stones for their garden," JC replied.

Tigger's eyes lit up as she crawled up onto the arm of the chair. JC didn't seem to mind the intrusion into his personal space and Simone hoped he wouldn't notice her watching them, trying to figure him out.

"Do you have a fairy garden?" Tigger asked.

JC shook his head, finishing off his own drumstick. "Do you?"

Tigger nodded and held up five fingers.

"Did you know that if you mix Jell-O powder and glitter together after it rains it can help them fly?"

Tigger slowly shook her head, focused wholly on the man. There was something about him that was mesmerizing to all females—any age—wasn't there? Too bad he was a big, burly, heart-smashing alpha under it all.

"Because, see..." JC shifted to face Tigger more fully. "If they get caught in the rain then their wings' special flying powder gets washed away."

Tigger gave him a somber look. "That's bad."

He nodded. "But usually what they do is they find a trail left by slugs—you know how they glitter and shine, but disappear after about a day? It's because the fairies collected the glitter. They use it to replenish their flying powder. But you can mix up your own if there aren't any slugs around to help."

"Really?"

He nodded again. "It's fairy magic."

"Tigger, that's enough," Daphne said, trying to save JC, and making Simone snap to. She'd become totally involved in their conversation again. "Why don't you come play Go Fish with me and Dot?"

JC waved her away. "It's okay."

Tigger was staring at the room's dark windows, which were rattling in the wind, their closed shutters clanging every so often. "Fairies hibernate."

"They do?" Simone asked from her spot across the spacious room.

"With the squirrels. They cuddle to stay warm," she added in a serious voice filled with regret, her focus back on JC. "But the squirrels like to eat their hair ribbons. And make their coats into nests. They aren't very good at sharing sometimes. I don't think they went to kindergarten."

JC chuckled and caught Simone's eye. She was struck by how he seemed to be an entirely different person while talking to Tigger. Gentle, kind and very real. There were no walls. Not even a hint of the expected jock mentality or that superior grin he'd flashed at Simone moments ago.

But this was good. She'd seen both sides early and wouldn't fall for him. There was no room in her plans to become confused over an attractive man such as JC. But he really needed to stop smiling and being so sweet to Tigger. It wasn't fair. He couldn't be so nice to the girl, lure her into liking him, then go back to being a big macho guy who wouldn't even say hello if he passed her on the street. The connection was going to mean too much to Tigger.

"Have you read the *Rainbow Magic* books?" he asked, head bent low to match Tigger's. "It's about little girls who are friends with fairies and get help from them. I think you'd really enjoy the stories if you haven't read them already."

Fairy books? Did his sweetness never end? This was so wrong. He needed to stop acting like the man Simone had dreamed about. Carefully, she crossed her arms, pinching the tender flesh on the inside of her arm. Nope. Not having a hormone-induced fantasy.

"She hasn't learned to read yet," Evander said gruffly, his own arms crossed, his brow furrowed. Simone smiled in relief. JC's act wasn't getting under just her skin, but Evander's, too. The men would suss him out, help her stay safe—or sane, or whatever it was she needed. Maybe an ice-cold shower.

"I know a few words, like *bat* and *cat*," Tigger said eagerly. "I could read them!"

"Maybe your mom could read them to you? Or, uh, Evander?" JC glanced at the big man somewhat doubtfully.

He gave a sharp nod.

"Right." Simone stood with her empty plate. Enough of the Mr. Nice Guy act. Time to get to the bottom of who he really was. "So? Beat anyone up lately, or have you been too busy learning about fairies?"

JC gave her a hurt look, the walls folding around him again. She could practically hear them clang and lock back into place, shutting her out so fully she almost had to take a step back.

"Simone..." Hailey said, giving her a funny look.

"You used to get into real knockdowns, didn't you?" Simone continued, determined to figure out what game JC was playing, to expose him for who he really was.

"Yeah, I did," he said, standing to face her. "Usually when close-minded individuals tried to place me and my family into a little box."

Simone gasped. "Are you implying I'm close-minded?"

He simply raised an eyebrow and turned back to Tigger. "Come on, kid. I'll show you some ribbon designs so you can help your fairies redecorate their hair come spring."

Simone glanced around the room, looking to see if anyone else was as outraged by the way he'd dismissed her. But everyone's gaze darted away. Okay, so she'd been a bit harsh, but she'd only been trying to protect Tigger.

"I am not close-minded," Simone said, her voice small.

JC gave her a "sure, sure" nod and went to retrieve his cell phone out of a snowsuit pocket, then handed it to Tigger.

Simone took her plate to the kitchen and returned to the living room a moment later to find Tigger utterly engrossed by the contents of JC's phone. Trying to ignore the fact that he'd won over the small girl in such a short period of time, Simone focused on building up the fire again.

JC came up behind her, his presence building a heat within her that wasn't related to the blaze she was stoking with the poker.

"Push the wood in farther or it could roll out," he said, as she added another log.

She faced him with a glare. "I know how to stack a fire."

"And create a fire hazard."

She growled at him and went back to rearranging the logs. Men like JC were bossy know-it-alls. They played games and weren't real. Men like him, she reminded herself, told her that she was incapable of love and that all she thought about was her business. Men like JC didn't see that she wanted the same things as everyone else. All of it. Family. Love. All the trappings of domesticity.

As she gave the log an extra jab she promised herself that even if it was the last thing she did, she was going to prove to JC that she was capable of love. She was going to love him and he was going to love her right back, without getting all insecure about how strong she was.

No, wait.

That was completely wrong.

She was having a baby. Her way. On her own. No JC and all his macho baggage. She didn't need a man. All she needed was to get home in time for her morning hormone shot.

No problem.

Except for that raging blizzard.

Chapter Four

Josh had Simone pegged. She was an unhappy, pretty little control freak who liked having things her way as well as lined up "just so." She probably dated men like Dustin and expected to change him.

When she'd got all in Josh's face about knowing stuff about fairies, he'd considered hiding out in a corner until the storm blew over, but had realized that, quite frankly, he didn't give a damn if she got her panties twisted in a knot. Her problem. Not his. She was probably used to having them wedged up her perfect little butt, anyway. If she had to reduce him to nothing more than a fighting lug so she could overlook him, then she was the one who had issues.

"Should we be rationing food?" Simone asked, as a few of the guys went back for seconds.

Control freak.

Josh adjusted the burning logs in the fireplace, carefully placing the screen across the opening when he was done.

"Who knows how long we'll be snowed in?" she added. "And while I know this is probably the last time all of us will be together for Christmas—"

"Why?" he interrupted, feeling irritated that she was being so bossy. There was plenty of food in the kitchen and they were all adults who were capable of solving a few food shortage problems without her dictating their lives. "Because we're going to suddenly starve to death?"

Environment Canada had said tomorrow was supposed to be nice after tonight's flurries and wind. Getting home wasn't going to be a problem.

"No, because everyone is moving on," she snapped.

Without her, obviously. Hence the knotted undergarments.

And while Josh admitted that rationing was likely a smart plan—just in case—at the moment he didn't feel like conceding any points to her controlling side. He wanted to win and he wanted to put her in her place, wherever that was.

"Afraid of a little storm?" he asked.

"You're still such an ass."

He let out a triumphant bark of laughter for getting under her skin so easily.

"Ass! Simone said ass!" Tigger squealed, bouncing in her seat at the card table.

"Tigger!" scolded Daphne.

"Sorry," Josh said.

"That's enough, Tigger." Evander placed his hand over the girl's. She quieted, her eyes gleaming as she looked up at the big man. That kid was life at its best.

Simone was glaring at Josh, hands on her curvaceous hips. She was sizing him up, likely trying to prevent him from getting under her skin any further. He watched her reassess her line of attack, bolster her defenses, and he admired her all the more even though he didn't want to.

"When will we get out of here?" Hailey asked. She smoothed her sweater over a small midriff bump, which he noted Simone watched out of the corner of her eye with...was that longing?

Why would someone like her want a kid? He couldn't even

begin to imagine her doting over a gaggle of offspring. Not unless she was a power mom. CEO of the color-coded family calendar.

He smiled at the thought. *That* he could see, actually.

But if she wanted kids, then why didn't she have them? She seemed like the type to make things happen, ripping through roadblocks as though they were made of crepe paper.

He shook away the thoughts. He didn't have time to get curious about a woman like her. He needed to keep her on the defensive so she didn't unearth his secrets, slaughter him wholesale in front of everyone.

"We'll catch our flight," Finian said to his wife, nuzzling her neck as she blushed and curled into him.

Josh had to look away, not quite sure where was safe. Everywhere he turned there were lovey-dovey couples getting friendly, and it made him feel like an intruder. No wonder Simone kept coming and sitting beside him. She needed escape and it was either with him, the surly teenager with strange-colored hair or bouncing Tigger. Personally, he'd choose Tigger, but then again, Simone didn't seem to appreciate fairies. They were probably too feminine. He let out a chuckle, quickly biting it back when she gave him a look.

"What?" she asked from a few feet away, adjusting photos that were hanging crooked on the wall.

"Nothing."

"No, what?" she insisted, abandoning her task.

"I was trying to imagine you doing something feminine."

She appeared taken aback. "I do feminine things all the time." She ran her hands down her sides, smoothing her outfit, and he immediately imagined her in very feminine, lacy, see-through attire.

"Sure," he said, not at all trying to hide the way his voice dipped low and gravelly with desire.

She flushed as though she'd been out in the sun too long, and glanced around the room, her desperate gaze finally landing on Melanie Summer, who was wearing a dress over woolly leggings. "I made that dress. By hand. That's feminine."

"You made that?" He darted a peek at the garment, which he'd noticed earlier. Melanie wore it as though it had been made specifically for her, from the print and color right down to the style and stitching. If Simone had made that, the woman not only had an eye for design, but some pretty serious talent and skills. Something he'd love to have.

She tipped up her chin. "I did."

"Really?"

"Yes, really." She gave an exasperated huff.

"She makes my woman look incredibly sexy," Tristen interjected, running a hand down his fiancée's back. "New dresses arrive all the time and we—"

"Shh!" Melanie scolded, head tipping down in pleased embarrassment.

"You need to start charging her for these. I'd pay thousands," Tristen said, nibbling Melanie's ear. He murmured, "I would have noticed you even without your stunning dress, you know."

Josh did his best to shut them out as their words became sweet enough to send a diabetic into shock.

He cleared his throat, wishing the fireplace needed more attending. "So you made that dress? By hand? That's a nice hobby." He tried to focus on Simone and not the annoying kissy noises that were coming from behind him.

"It's not a hobby, and I can do other things besides sew, you know," Simone said, her back straightening. "Being feminine doesn't get you ahead in this world."

"Okay." Josh let out a slow breath, realizing that while he'd been poking at her for fun, her hang-ups seemed to run deep. "Look,

I'm sure you do a great job of getting ahead in the world." He gave her a disarming smile, hoping she'd let it go.

She cocked her head to the side, and he found it difficult not to admire how sexy she looked when she was mad.

"What's that supposed to mean?" she asked.

All right. Time to pull the pin and let her explode so they could avoid each other for the rest of their sentence on Nymph Island. Finian moved behind Simone, pretending he needed the poker for the fireplace. He gave Josh a finger-across-the-throat signal.

"It means...don't pin your issues on me," Josh said, his voice displaying fatigue with their pointless fight.

Finian's eyes grew large and he playacted dying a horribly violent death. It was a wonder the man hadn't won an Oscar, and Josh tried not to appear amused by the comedy unrolling behind an unsuspecting Simone.

She stalked over to him. "Could you be any more condescending?"

"Probably, but I like how your throat gets all splotchy and red when you're annoyed. I think you'd lose the splotchiness if you got more upset."

He was right. That smooth skin was already being flooded by more red. This woman was a ball crusher and he happened to like his balls in a unpuréed form. That meant if he planned on coming out alive he needed to end it. End it now.

He loomed closer, certain he knew which final button to push. He'd get too near, make her uncomfortable enough with a few suave moves, and she'd avoid him until the end of time, righting his world once again.

She crossed her arms over her chest, holding her ground. "I don't like you." When he didn't respond, she jabbed him in the chest with a long fingernail, glossy with layers of perfect polish.

"You're not the first," he said, catching her finger, "and you won't be the last."

"You imply that because I'm a woman I'm weak and can't possibly have achieved anything worthwhile." She wrenched her finger out of his grip, her arm flying backward as he released it.

"Simone," one of the sisters warned.

"No," she said, focusing on Josh, "I know your type. You act all smooth and fun, but you can't take it when push comes to shove. You can't handle the tough stuff and you're not man enough to do what feels right in your heart."

He felt shaky, her digs striking chords of truth, and he was getting the feeling she'd go on all night—or at least until she had him strung up by his nuts, which wouldn't take long at this rate.

"You probably say you love someone, but when the chips are down, you can't handle a strong woman. You think you're a real man, but you're not."

Josh rubbed his forehead. "That's your issue, not mine."

"No it isn't, and I can see it all over you, plain as day. You're just like the others, so quit playing games with me. I know that look. I know what it says."

He decided to up his approach, since there didn't seem anything to lose, and she was starting to strike too close to home. He eased even closer, feeling like a primal cat tracking down his prey. Josh dragged his gaze up her body, allowing his eyes to fill with desire and sensuality. "And what is my look implying now?"

She gave a series of flustered blinks, her cheeks flushed.

The whole room had gone silent, and he was starting to wonder if he'd find himself seeking shelter in a snowdrift until the blizzard was over and he could escape.

"Tell me, Simone. Are you afraid of our chemistry?" Josh ran a hand down her arm. She shivered but didn't quite push away. Risking it, he tipped up her chin, aligning his lips with hers. He paused there, hovering over her, curious whether she would meet him halfway or whether the group surrounding them would break it up.

"You're a tease." She crossed her arms, not pulling away, that adorable flush spreading all the way to her ears.

"Yeah?"

"And I don't like you."

"You've already said that."

Knowing he should break contact, he tried to move away, but found he couldn't seem to release her. He must have taken a bigger bump to the head than he'd thought, because right now he wanted her to like him. A lot.

He knew better, though. Women like Simone were too much work to handle, making him fall back on his basic, dominant side when he knew he could be so much more. But right now, as the heat from the fireplace warmed them, all he could do was wonder what her lips tasted like. Salty? Like lip gloss? A perfect blend of something uniquely Simone?

"Just like in high school," she said quietly. "Try to make the girls swoon, then walk away laughing."

He kissed her lightly, his lips tingling with the electric pulse that came off her in waves. She tasted...like snowstorms and cherries.

He broke the kiss, delighted she'd allowed it. He murmured, "I'm not laughing."

Her dark eyes were black with consternation. "Neither am I."

Still holding her chin, he kissed her once more, quickly, wanting to see if that ticklish jolt would happen again when their lips met.

It did.

He made himself back away before he could wrap his arms

around her and claim her in a stupid move he'd likely regret for the rest of his miserable life.

"Well, uh, that was fun," Maya said, rolling her shoulders before giving everyone a big smile, attempting to draw attention away from the now dissolved fight. "Did you know Simone made my wedding gown? Gave me the sister rate—free."

"Enough about the dress, Maya," Daphne said with a grumpy frown, arms wrapped tight around her slight frame. "We've heard about it eight hundred times."

Josh blinked at the women, trying to get his head around the fact that he'd just tenderly hate-kissed Simone in front of everyone in an attempt to get her to eff off. What on earth had just happened?

He should never have come out here tonight. He wanted to hold Simone's hand and snuggle on the couch. Which was not his style. At. All.

He rubbed the bump on the back of his head and went to the kitchen for a beer, before changing his mind and snagging a bottle of iced tea instead. If the storm cleared up he'd have to leave—no matter the time of day—and would need his wits about him in order to do so safely.

The kitchen was freezing, but he took a moment alone to think. He *never* let a woman get that far under his skin. And so quickly. Simone had found buttons to push that he hadn't even known he had. How had she turned everything around on him?

"Right, well, did I tell you all I have plans for tomorrow?" Maya was saying in the other room. "And those plans do not include me being stuck on this island. All of us in this tiny living room all night trying to stay warm? Give me a real place to sleep." From the doorway Josh saw her playfully whack her husband on the shoulder. "Get us out of here, would you?"

Figuring it was safe to rejoin everyone, Josh drifted back to the spot in front of the fireplace, warming his hands, turning to face the group. He could feel Simone's presence beside him as surely as a touch. He glanced at her, but she looked away, down and to the left as though the flooring was suddenly of utmost interest. For a second he felt guilty. There was an air of vulnerability to her now, as though their fight had been about proving something important to herself and losing had set her back. He just about reached out to comfort her, to let her know it wasn't personal, when she straightened her shoulders and put on the visage of entitled, powerful woman again.

"Good idea on getting out of here," Simone said. "What do you have on tap for us, Mr. Connor MacKenzie?"

"Put in an order with Mother Nature, ladies," Connor replied drily. "It doesn't matter how many bucks I have, they won't do us any good in this weather."

"Oh, come on," Maya said with a pout.

"Spitfire..." Connor warned. But she grinned at him and he grabbed the back of her neck, pulling her in for a long, deep kiss that had everyone turning away to give them privacy.

Josh glanced around the large room. There were worse places the dozen of them could be stuck; and he knew, because he'd been stuck there. And given the chance, he'd always choose cold over too much heat. Forest fires did that to a guy.

"It's not so bad here," he said. The place was rustic, over a century old, but it had been built well and was standing the test of time like a trooper.

"It would be even better if it had a working flush toilet," Simone said.

"Fully winterized," Maya chimed in with a sigh. "Central heat, running water." She was ticking things off on her fingers and Josh got the impression she wasn't the cottage's biggest fan.

Simone added, "At least the generator hasn't crapped out yet, so we have electricity."

"The guys got us a new one last fall," Daphne said.

"That's why it's so quiet!" Simone exclaimed. "Nice work, men."

Josh bit his bottom lip, feeling like a damn puppy for wanting some praise from her, too. She had definitely worked her way under his skin.

"We could use heated bedrooms so Hailey could rest her back in a real bed tonight," Simone added.

Finian, Connor, Tristen, and Evander shared a look, and Josh realized they were up to something. He eased himself into a chair so that the sudden change in altitude wouldn't send the lump on his head throbbing, and waited for their surprise to unfold.

"What?" Maya demanded. "What was that look about? What did you do?"

"We," Connor began, glancing at the other men, who nodded their consent for him to continue, "got you a little something for Christmas."

"Is that what's in Evander's package?" Melanie asked. Pink rose up the big bodyguard's neck and he avoided eye contact with anyone in the group.

"I thought the generator was our gift," Daphne interrupted, watching Evander carefully, her body language suggesting that things might not be wonderful in their little paradise.

"It was, but there's more." Evander placed a hand on her hip, drawing her close.

The women were circling the men, eyes alight in anticipation of the upcoming surprise.

"What is it? What is it?" Tigger chanted, dancing around the room. Even Dot was looking curious, her head popping out of the manga book she'd been reading.

Simone leaned closer to Josh. "You drove a snowmobile here, right?"

He nodded, giving her a look. She knew full well he'd come on his sled. Did he have to worry about her taking off with it?

She glanced over at the occupied sisters. "I'll pay you to get me home by eight-thirty tomorrow morning if these monkeys can't get their helicopters and billion-dollar plans working by then."

"Yeah?" Josh lifted his eyebrows, assessing her. She smoothed her sweater over her chest, enhancing the smallness of her waist and the fullness of her breasts. He inhaled, trying to quell the stir her body was creating within him.

What was so important that she'd flip on a dime, turning him from enemy number one to an elite member of her inner circle? Were his kisses that amazing?

While he'd like to think so, he couldn't help but wonder what she was up to.

"Why?" he asked.

Her large eyes lifted to meet his and he felt himself soften at their quiet desperation.

Damn woman.

"Name your price," she countered. She flicked her hand impatiently when he didn't reply. "How much?"

Behind Simone the sisters gasped at what was surely some exorbitant gift.

"You can't afford me." As tempting as it was to enter her inner circle, Josh would have to be nuts to succumb. She was trouble and he'd do well to remember that.

"Try me," she challenged, her voice low.

Fine. Time to see how serious she was. If she was going to push, he was going to make it worth his while being stuck with her. "A thousand."

"Dollars?" she confirmed, giving him a little bit of sass.

Implying that his amount was a pittance and well below her expectations.

"If you give me attitude, two thousand." He crossed his arms over his chest.

Simone echoed his pose. "Three."

Josh turned his palms upward in question. What on earth kind of bargaining was that? He hoped she didn't do her own negotiations for those dresses she made. Then again, the Summer sisters had said she'd given them away.

The room emptied around them, leaving Josh and Simone alone. There was only one reason a woman would pay three thousand dollars for a twenty-minute snowmobile ride.

"Are you in trouble?"

She seemed taken aback before going on the defensive. "I need to be home by eighty-thirty. Can you make it happen or not?"

"If the helicopter can't come get us by then, I doubt it will be safe for us to make our way across the lake on a snowmobile."

"So you're not man enough?" she said, tossing her head in challenge.

A fight flared up inside him, but he reminded himself that a trip across the ice in sketchy weather wasn't worth anything if you didn't make it out alive.

"Well?" she prompted.

Simone Pascal was a piece of work. A beautiful piece of work.

But she was calling him a wuss. Not verbatim, but essentially that was the message. Josh felt the muscles in his jaw flex as he fought the mighty urge to show Simone just how much of a man he was.

But years of firefighting training had taught him to push those emotions aside. The ego. The history and scars from the past that made men do stupid things, putting themselves at risk—whether with forest fires or with women.

He stared down at Simone, wanting to run his fingers through her rich dark hair. She had pushed out her chest while making her pitch and he found his gaze drawn to their perfect curves. Irresistible. If she wasn't the exact opposite of what he needed, he'd probably try and get her into bed.

"Why are you willing to risk both our lives to get home by a certain time?" he asked.

"It's none of your business."

"Oh, I think it is."

"Can you or can you not?"

Why would a smart women take such a risk? Both in high school and over the past hour she hadn't struck him as a great risk taker. It was true she was the kind of woman who came along and crushed barriers that stood in people's way, but not without knowing all the angles first. She had single-handedly convinced the teachers of their high school to allow dances to be held again after a couple of Josh's buddies had become drunk and caused a scene. She'd been a hero.

But right now? The desperation radiating off her told him she might not have considered all the angles this time.

"Why?" he insisted.

"Can you do it or not?"

"It's risky."

"Do I need to look elsewhere?"

A loud voice in the back of his head shouted, *"No!"* And he was pretty sure it wasn't just because she was the type to take the snowshoes above the mantel and set off on her own to try and meet her goal—despite the dangers. Her mind was set and all he could do was cushion any possible blows that would come her way. He had to keep her safe.

"So?" she asked, pressing him for an answer. "Will you?"

"I'm your best bet, Simone."

She blinked and started as though she had been shocked, her gaze falling from his pectorals to the floor. Just as quickly, she looked up, meeting his eyes, judging his sincerity. "Is that a yes?"

"If whatever you need to do is worth risking your life for, then, yes, I will do my best to get you there while keeping you safe."

She nodded briskly, smoothing her hands over her locks, her long, graceful fingers capturing his attention. He imagined her getting onto the back of his snowmobile in the morning, wrapping her arms around his waist, locked together as they raced across the lake. She would feel good, and he knew his brain would keep him up all night imagining the feel of her curves molded against him. That and procuring scenarios where she'd have to straddle him, face-to-face, instead of sitting behind him.

He needed to get her and her sexy ass off this island before she crowbarred her way into his life.

She licked her lips, her mouth dropping open as she prepared to speak, and his groin tightened involuntarily.

"No," he breathed, trying to look away from her moist lips. "We don't go tonight. I make the calls."

Her brow furrowed.

"It's dark. There's a whiteout, which means we could get lost just trying to find the snowmobile. You still have twelve hours before you have to be home. We'll find our window out of here."

"Promise?" she asked softly, a rare vulnerability peeking through.

"Yeah. Promise."

The pinched expression that had increased during their conversation washed away and she stood on tiptoe, one hand against his chest. He froze, her scent locked into his mind as she gently brushed her lips against his cheek. She smiled, an electric hum hitting his core.

"Thanks."

There were no two ways about it. That woman was trouble.

THE MEN, IT TURNED OUT, had purchased electric heat for each of the bedrooms, so the Summers could start spending nights on Nymph Island during the shoulder season—which, quite frankly, was handy timing. Everyone in the cottage except Josh seemed to be rolling in cash, and now even Simone was offering him stupid amounts of it for a short snowmobile ride.

His head felt tight and he wasn't sure if it was the cumulative impact of the constant background throbbing of his goose egg or simply the fact that everyone around him seemed to be successfully pursuing the things they wanted to do with their lives and he wasn't.

Tigger had sneaked another juice box and Simone placed it on the mantel beside two others and flopped into the armchair opposite him. Why did she keep sitting beside him? He wasn't up for another damn fight with her. He got that it was difficult sitting with the lovebirds, who had taken over the whole place from the couch behind their armchairs to the card table and sitting nook, but he needed a break.

"I like this one!" Tigger called, waving his phone in the air. She was tucked into the window seat by the rattling shutters, studying photos of his accessories.

"Me, too," he replied, unable to focus on the moving device. "What do you do for a living? You make dresses?" he asked Simone, tending to the fire so no one else would mess with it.

Everyone seemed to toss logs in willy-nilly, sending sparks onto the extended hearth, then sweeping them up with a bristle broom. Talk about fire hazard. He'd had to stomp out more than one spark on the knotted rug at his feet. The worst of it was this place was essentially a pile of kindling waiting for a lit match to fall.

"Yes. And I have a boutique." Simone turned in her seat, addressing Connor. "Hasn't it cleared off yet? What kind of weather can helicopters fly in?"

"Afraid to pay up?" Josh joked quietly. He could still feel the burn of her kiss, where her lips had lingered when she'd thanked him only minutes ago. He had a suspicion he'd be enjoying the phantom sensation of her touch for hours, days, weeks.

"Not this," Connor replied.

"What do you sell in your boutique?" Josh asked, attempting to distract Simone into relaxing.

"I own it, run it, stock it," she replied simply, not answering his question. Her hands were pressed tight between her thighs, her shoulders hunched forward.

"And it does okay?" Josh was definitely getting the vibe that something was wrong in Simone's life right now. Was her business in trouble? Was that where the tension was coming from? He knew it couldn't be easy running a store, given the ebb and flow of tourists that ran through the local area. "I have some stuff I sell on Etsy and eBay."

He cringed internally. Why did he say that? Was he nuts? She didn't need to know about his creations. She was the last person who would understand him, and the first to make assumptions. She was the type who would mock his work and fail to understand who he was just because he made delicate hair accessories.

"It does fine," she said.

"She does art shows, too," Hailey added as she passed by, looking for something.

"Anything to get foot traffic." He understood that.

"It's on the main route through Port Carling. Traffic isn't an issue in the summer."

"Do you have much space for inventory?"

"It's a converted house, so yes."

Something familiar was trickling through his mind, setting off alarm bells, a tightness forming in his chest.

Wait a second... "Didn't a boutique in Port Carling just get a deal to expand and distribute their handmade dresses internationally?"

It had to be her. He'd almost reached out to that boutique owner, asking if they could form a partnership of sorts, but he'd chickened out at the last moment. Now he was glad he had. The last thing he needed was someone like Simone laughing at him, feeling sorry for him while being trapped in the same old cottage overnight.

"That was a few months ago," she said, her tone offhand, her glance flicking to the Summers and their men.

Son of a... Her boutique was obviously doing better than fine.

Josh felt his shoulders fall. Simone was the woman he needed to talk to if he wanted to bump things up to the next level with his hobby, turning it into a legit business. But she was the last woman he wanted to talk to. She was a superwoman, and everything was too fresh, too tender for him to deal with someone who could be so blunt, callous, and to-the-point with her criticism and advice.

"Her business is doing really well," Melanie said. "Her dresses are always perfect."

"Delectable," Tristen agreed, giving Melanie a kiss on the forehead.

"She was in the *Financial Times* a few weeks ago," Connor offered, quick to get in on singing her praises.

Instead of looking pleased and proud, Simone seemed almost bothered by the attention and ready to change the subject.

"Congratulations," Josh said.

She gave him a brief smile. "Thanks."

"What?" he asked. "You don't like the success?"

"It's fine."

She wouldn't meet his eyes. She was hiding something.

"You want more?" he prompted.

She let out a weary sigh.

"Too much attention then?" What made this woman tick? He almost hoped she found the spotlight too much, as he could identify with that. When he brought his fairy art and hair accessories into the Children's Burn Unit the kids always made such a fuss. It was a pleasure, a real reward, to see them enjoy his creations, but sometimes it was overwhelming. They were just ribbons, sequins, lace, and other fun bits glued or stitched together. Painstakingly. But they weren't going to change the world, and the assessing sidelong looks, along with the unwanted questions in the nurses' eyes, almost didn't make it worth it sometimes.

"The attention is fine."

"Yeah?" He reached over, tapping Simone's arm with his knuckles. "Then chill. Enjoy the ride." She was at the top of her game. What was there to worry about? It wasn't as if anyone would be looking at her as though she'd lost her mind for creating dresses.

"Chill?" She blinked at him twice and repeated, "Chill?"

"Yeah." Why did it feel as though he was fighting a long-term girlfriend and not an acquaintance? "Be happy."

She gave him a nasty scowl. "Who says I'm not happy?"

"Your face."

"Excuse me?"

Women. Everything was an insult when they were mad.

"You're obviously not." He glanced behind him, expecting some backup. But everyone remained silent, suddenly too involved in their card games, books, and other conversations to lend a hand.

Apparently Simone wasn't one to be messed with. Which meant he was going in, guns blazing, alone.

Goodbye, nuts. Nice knowing you.

"If you were happy and doing what you're supposed to be doing with your life you'd be overjoyed, and it would show on your face."

"And you're the poster boy for happiness and fulfillment?" She crossed her arms, giving him a look as if to say, *"I win."*

"Not in the least." He leaned back in his chair, taking a sip of his iced tea. "But at least I'm willing to admit it."

"Maybe I'm already doing what I want to do," she added, a hint of imp twinkling in her eyes.

Secrets. That woman had secrets.

"Then smile." He leaned forward, knowing he was pressing into her personal space again despite them being in opposite chairs.

She flashed him a lot of teeth.

"Not a snarl, a smile."

"You don't deserve a smile." She turned away in her seat. Point for Josh.

Hailey, swilling a hot toddy, tossed another log on the fire, laughing at Finian, who was making faces at Tristen's daughter, Dot. The two were in a battle, seeing who could make Tigger laugh the hardest. Someone had to be winning, as the kid was giggling like a demented hyena and about two seconds away from accidentally smashing his phone. Sparks flew onto the hearth and area rug before Hailey closed the screen.

"Good plan. Mix alcohol and fire," Josh snapped at her, getting up to take care of the live embers. They'd be royally screwed if this place went up in flames tonight.

Hailey stepped back, holding her drink closer to her chest. "It's not a *real* hot toddy. I'm pregnant." She gave him a look and stomped away.

Great. Way to go. Insult the hostess. He'd just bumped up the expiration date on his welcome.

"Sorry, sorry," he muttered sheepishly.

He readjusted the screen, ensuring sparks couldn't fly past.

"I've got this." Simone pushed it aside, hip-checking him out of the way to poke at the logs, adjusting them in what he grudgingly admitted was the way he would have if he hadn't been so worried about the place burning down.

"My hot toddy isn't real, either," Melanie said to the group with a shy smile. "I made mine with herbal tea."

"Why?" Simone asked hesitantly, as though afraid to hear the answer. Standing beside her, Josh could feel the tension radiating off her like heat waves.

"We're trying to have a baby."

Simone's forehead wrinkled and Josh wondered why she didn't seem more excited for her friend.

Tristen put an arm around his fiancée's shoulder. "We know we aren't married yet, but we don't care. We will be soon enough." He gave Melanie a look filled with so much love that Josh found himself wishing he could find someone who would accept him exactly the way he was: confused. And not following his dreams because he was a big chicken. Right. That would definitely be quite the woman. A great way to start a strong relationship, too, he'd bet.

He rubbed his face, dismissing his thoughts. A relationship ran the risk of pushing him off track right now, and for once he was finally allowing himself to create without censorship. Getting involved with someone would undoubtedly relocate that new ability to the back burner.

"Good luck. I hope it goes well for you," he said to the couple, trying to put the screen back in front of the now roaring fire. But Simone stood stock-still, her shoulders rounded down, blocking his way.

"Thank you." Melanie beamed at him and began chatting with Hailey and Daphne about babies, while Maya rolled her eyes.

"Simone, can you move, please?" Josh murmured.

"I know, okay?" she whispered back, still blocking his path.

"Know what?" he asked. She was making his head hurt more than the bump was.

"I'm okay with being a control freak." The strain in her expression was new and his instinct to take care of her kicked in, overriding his innate need for self-preservation. "I know it's not easy for men like you to deal with, but it's the way I am. It's who I am."

"I don't care if you're a control freak, Simone, but sometimes you're a danger to yourself. Do you get that?"

"Excuse me?"

"You're so determined to get out of here, you think you can take on this whiteout. It would eat up anyone—even me." He gestured to the windows, which now had snow packed between them and the shutters. Outside the wind howled, sending drafts through the large living room. "You need someone to take care of you or you'll end up making use of those in the dead of the night." He pointed to the old-fashioned snowshoes hanging above the fireplace.

She blinked furiously, her face a scary shade of red. "I do *not* need taking care of. And definitely not by the likes of you."

Her voice had a dangerous edge to it, and Maya quietly slipped from the room, taking Connor with her.

The red, blinking light in his mind warned Josh to back off.

"Move." He needed to put the screen back in place so more flying sparks didn't ignite the place.

Simone's delicate hands had wrapped into tight fists, ready to lash out. Fighting stance. Ready to protect herself. He echoed her posture, loving the way she narrowed her eyes in challenge.

God, he enjoyed a tough woman. Too bad they just about killed him every time.

"You know," he said quietly, "I haven't had so many fights with one person in such a short period of time since I was sixteen." A flash of anger seared him as he recalled battling it out with Austin Smith over Josh's father's metamorphosis into womanhood.

"Well, welcome to talking to a real person, buster. One who won't allow you and your wishes to rein her in."

"Who said anything about that?" More like try to rein in the crazy insecurities.

Simone pushed up her sleeves and leaned forward, ignoring her friend. "I doubt you've even paused to consider what we're up against out here. You think it'll all just get taken care of by magic, but so you know, we're stuck in a drafty cottage with not enough food, probably not enough gas in the generator to keep the electricity on all night for the bedroom heat, nor do we have enough wood stockpiled on the back porch. We have no cell or Internet connection and nobody gives a crap because they're under the haze of new love! These are problems." She smacked her right hand into her left palm. "Problems I can solve. So don't get in my face about thinking you're somehow stronger than me and that you have to take care of me. I can do just fine on my own."

The logs in the fireplace shifted and crashed, sending up sparks. Simone flinched and let out a squeak of pain. Without thinking, Josh yanked the straw out of two of Tigger's juice boxes lining the mantel and squeezed, sending dual streams of apple juice onto the live spark burning through Simone's tight jeans. Simone patted the burn and he wrenched her hand away, then tossed a nearby blanket over the spot, smothering it in case the liquid had missed its mark.

The logs snapped and cracked behind him, throwing off another shower of glowing sparks.

"Dammit! Someone put the screen in place!" He flung it in the general direction of the fireplace as Simone squealed again, dancing away from the hearth. Before he had a chance to process what he was doing, Josh had the woman bundled tightly in his arms and was standing on the veranda in the midst of the stinging blizzard, applying snow to the burn holes in her pants.

She struggled to escape his grip, but he held fast, pressing large handfuls of snow against her thigh.

"It's cold!" One of her feet had found purchase on the veranda, but he held the other leg against him, still applying snow. She curled into him for balance, arms around his neck, a warm spot against the frigid wind swirling around them.

"The sooner we get cold on your burns, the better."

He really needed to get back into structural firefighting and away from wildland fires. Rabbits, deer, and squirrels didn't regard him the way Simone was right now. Such dark, trusting eyes, it made a part of him grow. And not the part that usually came with gazing into a woman's bedroom eyes.

Something about holding Simone in his arms felt right.

"Damn you, Simone," he said, as he took her mouth in a kiss.

Chapter Five

Okay, this was nice.

JC had completely overreacted to the sparks that had burned through her clothing. Being the he-man he was, he'd jumped into action, carrying her away to save her from disaster.

And now he was kissing her with lips that were surprisingly soft and gentle, not pushy or demanding. All Simone's insecurities and fears washed away. It was a real kiss—not like earlier. This was a kiss between lovers; he was giving and taking, and her body thrummed with a need for more.

She liked it in all the wrong ways, and she reminded herself that she didn't need someone to take care of her. She didn't need a big burly alpha to rescue her from a little spark singeing her skin. She hated it when men swooped in, overreacted and assumed she couldn't handle things.

Didn't she? Didn't she hate that? Yes, she was pretty sure she did. She wasn't supposed to like anything JC did.

Not even one teensy tiny bit.

Right.

Except he was a *really* good kisser. Olympic athlete kisser. And he was warm, strong. Solid. Holding her safely against him, her leg propped at his waist as he pressed a handful of snow to her thigh. He was shelter in the raging blizzard that swirled around them, lifting her hair and chilling her with its frigid breath.

This kiss was even better than the stupid fight-kisses he'd given her in front of everyone, trying to get her to stand down. Little did he know that she was totally onto him.

He nibbled her bottom lip and she barely held back a moan of contentment. It had been so long since she'd kissed someone so slowly and deeply, and even though her fingers were starting to hurt from the cold she didn't want JC to stop. Ever.

Which meant he was a very dangerous man.

She liked danger, didn't she?

She was pretty sure she did. She must, because only a fool wouldn't enjoy this.

"I'm sorry," JC said, finally breaking away.

"For what?" she whispered, trying to prevent herself from rubbing her cheek against his strong chest. She was certain it would feel divine. Maybe she could sink against him for a while and allow someone else to stand guard in her life so she could rest. Just for a little bit.

"For, uh, saving you. Not that you need to be saved," he added quickly.

She practically purred against him. He was a fast learner, avoiding her personal land mines with a deftness that could be fun. In bed.

Her leg was still in his grip, wrapped around him as though they had stopped dancing midtango.

"Sometimes a woman needs to be saved," she murmured, giving up her internal battle and allowing her cheek to rest against his warmth.

Definitely time to get out of his arms. The hormones were turning her into a swooning fool.

Simone did not do swooning. She did not do fool.

She did strong, reliable, and independent.

Their exhaled breath barely had time to form moist clouds

before the vicious wind whipped it away. Yet they stared at each other for a moment, their earlier bickering forgotten. There was a kindness, a gentleness in JC's eyes, and a protective vibe came off him, leaving her feeling safe as well as quiet inside. Relaxed.

Different.

He wasn't really a big macho man, was he? That was just an outer coating, like a garment he donned to face the world. In fact, he was...

Simone frowned in thought. What *was* he?

Well, whatever he was, he was striking a lot of chords that had so far not been strummed by any of the men she'd dated.

Which meant he wasn't who she'd thought he was. And yet he was still rescuing her.

What did that mean?

"Are you okay?" His voice had taken on its earlier huskiness, and her body suddenly took notice of the ways he was male, the freezing wind forgotten.

"I'm fine," she answered. "Is your head okay?"

"I'll survive." He removed the handful of snow he'd been pressing to her leg. Her body heat had melted some and the area felt icy, exposed to the wind, sending shivers ripping through her body.

"You're always fine, aren't you?" he murmured, setting her gently on her feet.

"Always."

He kept an arm around her ribs as though needing to keep her close. Her arms remained around his neck, preventing him from breaking the half embrace. She liked this side of JC and wanted to discover more of it, fearing that if she let go she'd lose this exclusive glimpse.

She shivered again as the bitter wind whipped between their bodies, stealing the heat they had built up together. She snuggled into him instead of heading back inside as a rational woman would.

"You're cold." He reached to open the door like a gentleman, and in a flash she understood why women loved the gesture. Usually it drove her nuts, but in this moment she knew he was simply looking out for her and that the move came from a caring place, not superiority or chauvinism.

"And you're..." She stopped him from moving, trailing a finger down his chest as she tried to place what it was about him that differed from her expectations. His body trembled and he caught her finger, causing her to snap to. She was being a flirt and happily slipping into the role of woman in distress.

"You're unexpected," she said, hustling inside when he opened the door. She yanked him in with her so she could slam it behind them. "It's damn cold out there."

She tried to shake off the chill and slowly discovered that everyone in the living room was staring at the two of them, jaws slightly unhinged.

Josh gave Simone a quick, uncertain glance, combing a hand through his short blond locks. "Sorry, I overreacted. I'm a firefighter. Sparks. Burning through clothing. Everything's all right now."

He leaned over, reaching for Simone's leg to check the damage, and she let out a squeak as his touch sent lightning crackling through her nervous system.

"Are you all right?" He took a step closer as she backed away.

"Fine. Just cold. Your hands are cold." She gave a smile that felt forced and raced to the fireplace, before changing her mind and tearing into the bathroom, where she locked herself in. There was no running water and no heat in the small room. A stupid place to run to. But it was the only private place in the old structure and she needed time to collect herself.

"Are you okay?" Hailey called through the door.

"Yeah. Um..." Simone quickly whipped down her pants. "Just checking the damage." She was fine. Her legs were cold, pink, and the small burns wouldn't even think of blistering, thanks to Josh's speedy application of snow.

Hailey tried the knob. "We might have something we can put on it."

"Uh, no! I'm fine. Really. Just overreacted." She yanked her pants up again, terrified that Hailey would pop the old door's lock and see the bruise on her hip from the day's earlier hurried injection.

"Are you okay? For real? You seem—"

Simone pulled open the door. "Fine! See? Ta-da!"

JC was at the fireplace, sweeping up ashes, one eye on Simone as though he knew all that she was hiding. He set the screen carefully in front of the fire and said to all, "We need to keep the screen in place at all times."

This guy telling everyone what to do? Not the man she'd been kissing only moments ago.

It was all an act, wasn't it? Despite his possible soft side, his nose would still get bent out of shape if he saw her bank account. She didn't have time for dented egos, didn't have time for men like him.

"Come join us for a round," Finian called to JC, holding up a deck of cards.

Simone crossed her arms, waiting for her own invitation. Was this a guys-only game? She happened to be a fantastic, utterly ruthless poker player.

Minutes later Maya pulled a grumbling Simone aside, her finger darting between her and Josh, her voice none too quiet. "What's going on?"

JC, who was organizing his freshly dealt hand, stilled.

Simone raised an eyebrow at her friend. "As in the fact that they didn't ask us if we wanted to play?"

"Want us to deal you in, Simone?" Tristen asked, head bent over his cards, not looking up. The man was a divorcé and careful when women got ticked off. However, right now it only added to Simone's frustration. She wanted him to ask *before* they dealt, not after she made a fuss. She knew she was being an irrational female, but dammit, men had made her this way. It was their fault for making assumptions about her based on gender.

Daphne came closer. "You two have this..." She waved her hands in the air as though trying to get a sense of Simone's aura. "... this energy."

"No, we most definitely do not."

"It's because you both rescue people." Hailey piped up from her spot on the long window seat, where she was playing Go Fish with Tigger.

One kiss and the sisters thought the two of them were going to be heading down the aisle. Just because Simone could still feel the heat and pressure from his lips and wanted more didn't mean the kiss had actually meant something.

Kisses with players such as JC never meant anything.

"Rescue people?" Maya said, waking up her laptop. She was becoming just as bad as Simone—working all the time, although at least Maya was better at not blocking out the entire world around her once she got down to business. Simone had once missed her neighbor's house burning down because she'd been so involved in a proposal she'd been writing.

"He's a firefighter—obvious—and Simone is always solving everyone's problems. They're both fixers."

JC was giving Simone a thoughtful look.

"We're not compatible," she said, crossing her arms. "I don't go for the rescuing type. Too macho and pushy."

"That's okay," JC replied. "I prefer my women to be more open and accepting. Less prickly."

Simone let out a bark of laughter, ignoring Daphne's murmured advice about accepting their connection. "You prefer your women to be pliable and big breasted, that's what you prefer. The dumber, the better. Boss them around and then rescue them at every turn. It would kill you to add some yin to your yang."

"Sometimes a woman needs to be saved," he said, his voice flat as he mocked her earlier words.

Simone gasped, stepping forward, ready to fight. How dare he throw that moment back in her face!

"You seem to prefer the kind of man you can walk over," JC stated. "A man without cajones of his own. A man you can boss around and who will stand down at every raised word. You don't want a man, you want a lapdog." He slammed his cards on the table.

"Love, light, and forgiveness." Daphne gave them worried glances as though she was watching a pencil-pushing office worker try to diffuse something nuclear. "Evander, help."

The big man was up in a flash, following JC, who had stormed over to Simone. Evander kept his distance, but seemed ready to tackle him if need be. God, she loved her friends.

"Simone!" Tigger called excitedly. "Use the trick I showed you at my mom's birthday party!" She made a hugging motion with her arms, then hunched her shoulder, suggesting Simone should bind JC's legs together, then knock him down.

Simone sauntered toward him. "You feel threatened whenever it looks as though a woman might have bigger balls than you."

JC was close, his breath warm on her face. "You think you know me?"

"I know your type."

"And what is my type, exactly?" He crossed his arms yet again, giving her a look that made her doubt herself. He'd revealed an unexpected side when they were outside, and while it had taken her off guard, she knew it couldn't be real. It had to be an act to get her into bed. She'd fallen for it in the past with other men and had learned her lesson. There was no reason to relearn it.

Simone jabbed his chest with a finger, secretly loving and yet hating the way it felt: all muscle. "Alpha. Dominant. Protector. Macho. Male."

"Aren't you paying Mr. Alpha Dominant Protector Macho Male three grand to get you home by eight-thirty tomorrow morning?"

Simone clenched her jaw, angry that he'd mentioned their deal in front of the others.

"Well!" Connor said with a delighted laugh. "Simone's finally spending her signing bonus. Three grand for a Ski-Doo ride! You're right, Daphne, there must be a connection there."

"It's not like that," Simone snapped.

"Macho man is fine when you're stuck," JC continued, "but otherwise I'm not good enough for you? I'm just a thorn in your independent side. Why are you so afraid of accepting help from me?"

"I'm not afraid."

He leaned closer, his manly scent tantalizing. "I think you're afraid you'll lose control."

"Signing bonus?" Maya asked.

"Lose control?" Simone laughed. "You think your kisses are *that* amazing?"

"Signing bonus?" Maya repeated. "For what?"

"It's nothing," Simone said, realizing everyone was staring at her.

"Nothing? Don't be modest, this is huge," Connor said, not picking up on her reluctance to share the news. "She sold her patterns and entire brand to a major designer. Three-million-dollar contract." He snapped his fingers. "Just. Like. That."

The room filled with gasps and cheering, and Simone closed her eyes. *Nice going, Connor.*

"Sorry, was it a secret?" He looked so worried that she had to smile and let it go, pretend everything was fine even though this was going to open up the floodgates to every secret she had.

"Your whole brand?" Maya squealed, her jaw dropping open. "But what will you do?"

She gave a feeble shrug, knowing Maya understood the implications of what she'd done—sold her entire livelihood. Simone could no longer produce designs in her own name as she'd sold the rights. Anything new she created couldn't be sold unless under a different name. She would be starting over.

She was changing her life and the Summers wouldn't understand. She hadn't had time to prep them for this. And look at their lives—there was no way they could understand. They had everything and she had...nothing now. Nothing but hope and a possibility that kept slipping out of reach whenever she grabbed at it.

"Simone?" Connor asked, looking worried.

"No, it's good." Her voice was too high-pitched. Too strained. "Just waiting for the right time to announce it, that's all. So many fun announcements lately." She gestured to Hailey's growing belly, and Maya and Connor, who had eloped.

"Is Kmart still a secret, too?" Connor asked.

Could the man *not* give her a break? Simone pressed her hands flat against her legs so she wouldn't bunch them into telltale fists.

"What happened with Kmart?" Daphne asked.

"She sold the subsidiary line of dresses she designed for Melanie," Connor said proudly.

"Why didn't you didn't tell us?" Hailey demanded, her eyes wide with excitement.

"Oh, you know...just business stuff. Nothing as exciting as babies or marriage."

A round of hugs and toasts were made and Simone caught JC's eye as she turned to clink her teacup against Tigger's juice box. He gave her a look that was surprisingly understanding. She glanced back at him, wanting to see it again, confirm that it had been real, but the look was gone.

She couldn't figure it out, but she wasn't even mad at him any longer, despite having wanted to rip his throat out only a moment ago. Was it just the hormones, or something else? Whatever it was, she needed to get away, because being around him made her feel as though she was lost in a carnival. Enjoying a sweet and smooth carousel ride one second, pulling punches in the haunted house the next.

"Well, I can't wait to see what you do with your boutique in the spring seeing as you've sold the rights to everything you used to sell in there," Melanie said, smoothing out her handmade dress.

"What will be your new direction?" Maya asked. "Art gallery? Kids' clothes?"

Simone fidgeted with her cup of herbal tea, hoping someone would change the topic before she was forced to reply.

"Simone?" Melanie gently touched her shoulder.

"I sold it."

Gasps of surprise filled the room and JC started laughing. At first it was a light chuckle, but soon became an uproar, so loud and unnerving that Simone wanted to walk over and sock him in the jaw just to shut him up.

"It's not funny," she snapped.

"What?" Maya sputtered. "But...what are you going to do?"

"Just...something new," Simone said.

"What is it?"

"A...a lifelong project."

"And?"

"Let's just say it's a matter of now or never."

The sisters were silent; the men drifted back to their game of poker.

"Whose turn is it?" Tristen asked.

"Why do you have to be home by a certain time on Christmas morning?" Melanie murmured. Of course the lawyer had noted that little tidbit and had to bring it up again.

"I want to be with my mom."

"Badly enough to spend three thousand dollars?"

"Yeah, why the time crunch?" JC asked, and she shot him a glare. Not. Helpful.

"A flight somewhere?" Hailey wondered.

"You're getting married!" Daphne squealed, hands clasped hopefully beneath her chin.

"Are you freaking kidding me?" Simone cried. Her inner bitch was ready to pop up and start taking names and numbers. Stupid hormonal roller coaster. But she'd rather be a bitch than cry. And she'd been close to that a moment ago. No crying. No pitiful looks. She could apologize later for being snarky, but you couldn't take back pity when you spilled tears.

"What's wrong with marriage?" Maya asked.

The woman was a glowing new bride. She wouldn't understand. In fact, none of the females in the room would.

"You're such a catch," Daphne said. "And pretty. Smart. Determined and independent. Why won't you accept love and marriage?"

"Daphne, it's not about accepting it." Simone avoided looking at JC. "Who am I going to find to marry me?" She hated the way her voice sounded so choked up. She needed to shut up, but she was on the downward thrust of the hormonal roller coaster and gravity was pulling the words from her, leaving her powerless to stop them. "How much time have I spent on this island that's supposed to have magical superpowers, and yet I'm still single? You say I'm an honorary Summer sister, but obviously the magic prefers bloodlines." She threw up her hands, then rubbed her eyes, defeat closing in on her. "It doesn't matter. I don't know why I even care. Men and I are like oil and water. Nobody is going to love me. Nobody that I don't make myself. So what's the point?" She drew a shaky breath. "I give up. I don't need a man for anything, so why am I even talking about this?"

She dropped into a chair, feeling such turmoil she wanted to stomp out into the blizzard and scream and scream until her throat was as raw as her heart.

The room was silent for a long moment, then Hailey said, "Oh. My. God. Your secret lifelong project is a baby."

"You're adopting at 8:30 a.m.? On Christmas Day?" Daphne asked.

"Courts aren't open," Melanie replied.

"Who's the dad?" Evander inquired.

"I'm going to be an auntie?" Tigger asked, bouncing around, trying to catch up with the scrambling adults.

"You sold *everything*?" Maya was sputtering. "For a baby? Oh, geez. I think I'm going to throw up." She pushed her husband aside. "No, really. Barf coming through."

"Don't use the bathroom!" Hailey called, as her sister headed toward the nonfunctioning toilet.

"A sperm donor?" Melanie asked.

Simone gave a brave nod. "Yeah."

"You're getting the baby batter tomorrow?" Finian asked with a frown.

"No, it's Christmas," Hailey said, waving him away, her focus solely on her friend.

"A hormone injection," Daphne suggested, glancing at Simone for confirmation. "You have to stay on schedule."

Melanie gave her a look so filled with sympathy that Simone had to blink away tears.

"Designer baby?" Maya said, joining them again with a plastic trash can in hand. "I can see you doing that, actually."

"Oh, quit being dramatic." Hailey pushed the tub away from her sister's face.

"But what about love?" Daphne asked, sitting on the arm of a nearby chair as though the very thought had sapped her ability to stand.

"Can I name the baby?" Tigger said. "I have a book of fairy names. Priscilla is pretty." She turned to JC. "You can choose the middle name."

"Thanks for thinking of me, princess," he replied, ruffling her curls. "But I think Simone will want to name her little one."

"What's the dad look like?" Tristen asked. "Is he smart? Nice? And why is he giving away his sperm? Or selling it?"

"You're going to raise this kid? Alone?" Finian crossed his arms as though he was prepared to yank the decision from her hands if he felt it should be done. Ever since he'd revamped his bad-boy movie star image with Hailey's help he'd grown incredibly protective of anyone close to her. Which was sweet. Unless he tried standing in her way. In which case Hailey better not count on his ability to have more kids.

"She has money, apparently. So why not?" Maya said drily.

"I'm doing this," Simone stated. "Okay? I've thought about it long and hard. So either tell me it's a fabulous plan or shut up and move aside."

The sisters leaned back as if one connected unit.

Simone bit back tears, the medical facts explaining her decision stuck in her throat. She really *was* doing it alone. They didn't understand. Not everyone found love as they had. Not everyone had their lives fall into place. Some people had to work their tails off and they still didn't get everything.

JC moved to her side, his touch like a spark; it flared, burning like a lit fuse, streaking through her, looking for a place to explode.

"I'll get you home on time, Simone. You can count on me."

She nodded, knowing he was the one person she shouldn't lean on, but the one person who would get her through.

SIMONE SIGHED, STUFFING THE soiled paper plates in a trash bag to take back with them whenever the storm decided to let up. She didn't know what to think of JC stepping in to help. She supposed her acting like a damsel in distress spoke to his alpha rescuer side. It didn't really matter—her pride could take the hit if he got her home in time.

The wind rattled the shutters and whistled through the odd crack in the cottage's walls. At least the new generator seemed to be holding up despite the raging storm. She glanced around the kitchen, aware that if she could turn off a few more lights the machine might be able to power the electric heat for the entire night without running out of gas.

Someone short hugged her from behind. Daphne. "I think it's great you want to add a child to this world. You'll be a good mother."

"I hope so."

Daphne had always made motherhood look simple, even though Simone knew being a single mother hadn't always been easy for her.

"You'll do fine. And the fact that you won't have to worry about money or working will make it that much better."

"As long as my brain doesn't turn to mush." Simone laughed, fighting panic at the thought of sitting around with a baby, no career, and ignoring dress design ideas that came to mind. Plus going from superwoman to stay-at-home mom was such a sudden shift in speed she hoped it didn't break her internal drive's transmission.

Maya came bustling into the room. "Okay, so what's this really about? Can we talk about left field? You're on top of your game and have worked so hard to get there. You're landing incredible deals I'd commit murder for. You can't just drop it all for a *baby*."

"Too late." Simone tied the trash bag closed.

"You're already pregnant?" Maya frowned, looking to Daphne for an explanation.

"No."

"You didn't add alcohol to your drink tonight," Melanie said from the doorway.

"I'm trying to stay as healthy as possible, because last month's insemination didn't work."

"Oh, honey." Daphne gave her a hug. "Why didn't you tell us you were going through all of this?"

"You've all been busy and this was sort of last minute for me."

"How could this be last minute?" Maya asked.

"Everything's sold now," Simone said, steering the conversation away from the medical aspect, "and I transfer the last of my business and shop next month."

"But you're not even pregnant. What if you can't get in the family way?"

"Maya!" Daphne scolded.

Simone paused, trying to fight off the doubt that had niggled at her on more than one occasion. What *would* she do with herself if she couldn't get pregnant? She had planned the next nine months thinking her first insemination appointment would work, and it hadn't. Now she was ready for an adventure that might not come to fruition.

No, don't think about it. Stay positive.

She shrugged as though it didn't matter. "Everything just lined up for me to sell. I couldn't wait."

"Meant to be," Daphne said with a contented sigh. She gave Simone an extra squeeze.

Hailey, who had come up behind Melanie, asked, "Why now? Maya's right—your career is skyrocketing and you're not even thirty yet."

"What if you meet the right man?" Melanie interjected.

"If he is the right man," Simone said, pointedly looking at Daphne, "then he will love me even if I do have a child."

Daphne gave a nod.

"You really want a family?" Melanie asked. "No career?"

Simone swallowed hard. "I didn't sell everything off on a whim."

She knew that once you added too much to your paper plate at the banquet of life, your plate began to sag and you ended up with sweet-and-sour sauce on your new suede pumps. With big projects you had to do them one at a time. You could have it all, just not all at once.

"Well, I'm sure you'll get a baby one way or another," Maya said.

"Why is this last-minute? Is it because you got a good offer?" Melanie asked.

Simone took a deep breath, willing herself not to break down as she spilled the truth. "I have cysts that are choking off my ovaries. They are being removed in a few months and it might damage my womb."

Daphne's hand flew to her mouth and the other sisters gave her such sympathetic, horrified looks that Simone went back to dealing with the garbage.

"Why don't you get your eggs frozen?" Maya suggested a long moment later.

"It's not my style. I mean, I have in case, but I don't plan on using them. I'm doing this now, my way."

"Well, good luck, sister." Maya reached over and gave her a massive hug.

Within seconds, all the Summers were hugging her and whispering supportive phrases, and Simone felt bad for not giving them enough credit.

"I really couldn't have guessed any of this," Hailey told Simone. "But I'm excited for you. I haven't quite got my head wrapped around it, but I think it'll be good." She gave a not-quite-convincing smile.

"If you need anything, anything at all," Daphne said, "let me know. I don't have any of my baby stuff anymore, but I know about colic, morning sickness and all that stuff."

Hailey suddenly let out a squeal and gave a little bounce. "Our children might be in the same class! What if they're best friends? I'm so excited." She gave Simone another hug, blinking away tears.

Simone bit her bottom lip, trying to remain stoic, not quite having realized just how much she'd needed to know the Summers would be there for her, supporting her.

"It's all going to be okay, isn't it?" she asked, looking from sister to sister. They gave her reassuring smiles, just before the generator, with no forewarning, died, plunging them into darkness.

Chapter Six

Josh, glad a sharpshooter such as Simone hadn't joined the poker game, was about to win the entire stack of toothpicks set in the middle of the card table when the lights went out.

"Oh, man," Connor said from Josh's right, his features faint in the light from the fireplace. "Damn generator. Doesn't anything work the way it's supposed to these days?"

"Out of gas?" Finian asked.

"I'll go check." Evander's chair scraped back. "Tigger? You okay?"

A glow in the corner of the room highlighted the girl's soft features as she continued to play with Josh's phone. She waved the lit-up device under her chin, making ghostly noises. "Am I scary?"

"Very," Evander confirmed. "Everyone okay?"

The women had been chatting in the kitchen when the lights went out, and the sound of hands trailing along the rustic wood paneling filled the room as they returned to the living room. "Yeah, fine." It was Simone.

Josh was surprised at the relief he felt upon hearing her voice. She was probably the last female on earth he needed to worry about, and for some reason that made him worry about her all the more.

Connor flicked on a battery-operated lantern just as the women turned on several flashlights.

Evander pulled a black woolen cap low over his forehead, giving his scarred face a lean, serious look in the firelight's shadows. Josh usually felt as though he could take any man in a given room, but the bodyguard had a vibe that even Josh knew not to mess with. Plus he still didn't know what had been in the "life or death" package and whether it had any bearing on tonight.

Evander shrugged into his parka and Josh said, "I'll go with you." When the big man gave him a look, he added, "I can hold the flashlight."

Simone handed him a massive light. "Don't freeze your little chestnuts off."

"Thanks. But for the record, they *are* bigger than yours. More like coconuts."

"I wouldn't place any bets just yet," Maya muttered, handing him a toolbox.

"You should probably get that checked out," Simone said. "Only egos should be swollen, not nuts." She gave his crotch a discerning look and he refrained from shielding himself with the toolbox.

Connor came outside with the two men, cursing as the unrelenting wind hit them full force. "It's colder than a witch's tit out here." He shuddered and hunched further into his parka. The gusts whipped against them, then up over the side of the cottage, creating a lip of snow that hung off the edge of the roof, threatening to dislodge itself on them and the silent generator.

Josh shone the light over it, assessing the wisdom of standing under the frozen overhang. Deciding it was likely safe, he followed Evander and Connor, who had cut through a massive drift that had sculpted itself around the generator like a frozen wave.

"I don't think it's been tampered with," Evander said, gazing around the generator, on the lookout for tracks in the snow.

Connor shot Josh a sharp look when he opened his mouth to ask why anyone would come mess with their source of power.

"I think we're okay here," Connor said. "We're safe."

Evander gave a curt nod and stared at the inert chunk of yellow metal, likely as relieved as Josh that snow hadn't encased the machine, but rather had curved around it. Hopefully, the drifts were doing the same thing down on the lake, so he wouldn't have to dig out his snowmobile come morning. Josh trailed his flashlight over the generator, which was shiny and new and seemed to have no good reason to stop if the gas gauge was correct. He reached out a gloved finger and tapped it.

"It should run for eight to twelve hours on a tank," Connor said.

Josh handed the flashlight to him and, trailing a hand against the side of the cottage so he wouldn't get lost in the darkness, grabbed a shovel off the back porch. He returned, digging out a larger space in the blowing snow for Evander to work. Josh knew quite a bit about machines, but was reluctant to jump in before he was invited or was certain he could actually help. If Evander wanted to fix it and be the hero, that was fine by him. Josh didn't have a woman inside who he had to prove himself to. Especially not Simone, with those large, dark eyes of hers.

Tristen and Finian had come out to help and Josh suddenly found himself surrounded by four men in the small, shoveled circle.

"You need to be careful with Simone," Connor said.

"What do you mean?" Josh replied, on guard.

"She's going through a lot of big life changes right now."

"I get that."

"I'll be the one who safely delivers her home in the morning,"

Connor added, the wind stealing the force of his words as it swirled around them, already filling in the cleared space, a few fistfuls of snow at a time. In an hour it would be as though they had never shoveled it out.

"Okay." Josh widened his stance. "But if the weather isn't completely safe for your helicopter, there's no way in hell I'm letting her get into it. Nothing is worth her getting hurt."

He knew they were fighting words and that he might find himself headfirst in a drift as a result, but he needed these men to know that he had Simone's best interests at heart—even though she was the most difficult and annoyingly beautiful woman he'd ever laid eyes upon.

"None of us will," Evander said.

"She's one of the family," Finian added.

"And this family sticks together," Tristen stated.

Josh took in the determined set of their jaws and the way they all knew their lines within the little play that was unfolding. He pitied the man Tigger brought home as her first boyfriend. And yet, at the same time, he completely and utterly understood it. He felt the same way about Dustin sniffing around his sister, and she was a grown woman.

"We take care of our own," Tristen added.

But their interests were split and they weren't able to give Simone the unbiased attention and care she deserved. A powerful sense of possessiveness washed over Josh, settling deep into his bones. It was stronger than anything he'd felt in all his years, and he knew without a doubt that he needed to be the one to take care of her. That he was the only one with nothing to lose by pushing her back when she needed it the most.

"I would never do anything to hurt Simone, but if she chooses to ride on my sled, she's my responsibility. You have your own families to take care of." He continued, "She's going to do something stupid with that damned iron will of hers. You know that, I know that. I have a lot of experience saving people, and she's the type who'll put herself in even greater danger rather than allow someone else to help her. So while I know you have her best interests at heart, understand that I will cross you if I feel she needs me."

Evander reached forward and Josh forced himself not to dodge the incoming blow. But instead of punching him, the man grabbed Josh's hand and pumped it up and down. "Understood."

Tristen slapped Josh's shoulder. "Love is a tricky thing, isn't it?"

Josh cleared his throat and crossed his arms. "It's not love."

Tristen laughed and returned to the cottage with Finian, who gave Josh a knowing smile over his shoulder before disappearing into the darkness. Connor, hot on their heels, bellowed with laughter, Josh not quite catching the joke.

"What?" he asked Evander, who was grinning at him.

"Good luck. You're going to need it," Tristen called from the darkened doorway. "Evander, you have this machine under control, right?"

For a split second Josh considered that the breakdown may have been scheduled in order for the men to chat with him, but seeing the serious look on Evander's face as he contemplated the silent machine, he crossed the idea from his mind. This was real.

"I'll call if I can't figure it out," the bodyguard said, squatting as he got down to business.

"I didn't hear it chug," Josh offered. "I think there must be a broken connection." The generator was barely ticking with heat, which meant it was quickly cooling down and the metal would soon be killer on their bare hands if they had to do any serious work.

Evander said nothing, but began checking wires and hoses.

"What was in the envelope?" Josh asked, curious about the oh-so-important delivery that had got him stranded here.

"Sorry about that. I overreacted."

Josh's free hand instinctively went to the lump on the back of his head. He pulled up his snowsuit's hood, burrowing into its heat. "No problem."

"Daphne and Tigger were in danger this past summer, and while everything is good now, I guess I'm still not quite over it."

"Understandable." Josh waited, wondering if Evander would reveal what was in the package. They continued inspecting the machine.

"Any chance it overheated? That drift had it fairly closed in," suggested Josh.

At the same moment, Evander said, "It's a ring."

"Yeah?" Josh asked encouragingly.

"Not sure she will say yes, though."

"Why's that?"

More silence. Josh wiggled a loose wire, then tried restarting the machine. No luck.

"Daphne and Tigger have lived with me and my mother since August. I'm listed as one of Tigger's emergency contacts at her school."

"You're family."

"Yeah, family." The man's voice was filled with warmth and a sense of wonder. "I think it's been good for all of us. My mom's been battling cancer and having Tigger in our life is a great distraction. The doctor say she's doing amazingly well and even gave her permission to travel to my brother's for the holidays."

"That's good."

"Yeah. It's just..."

Josh waited quietly for the man to continue.

"Daphne's been independent for so long I'm not sure she wants to be tied to someone. The Summers—and that includes Simone—are all very independent women."

"I've noticed." Josh had also noticed they seemed okay with being cozied up to the men in their lives.

"I'd planned to ask her tonight and had it all figured out, but..." Evander's shoulders stiffened.

"But what?" Josh asked softly, knocking the snow off a connection so he could check it.

The man shook his head. "It's nothing."

"Well, you won't know unless you ask," Josh said, looking for something else that might be causing issues with the generator.

"Daphne's seemed different lately. Lost in her own world. I got caught up in the idea that maybe I was good for them. Sorry, it's not your problem."

Josh was starting to feel as though he was in over his head—with both the conversation and the generator. "I'm sure you're good for them."

Evander tried starting the machine and cursed when it remained stubbornly silent.

"What do you have on your phone that's so interesting, anyway?" Evander was gruff, brisk and, Josh could see, hurt. Slowly, it dawned on him. He had been monopolizing the man's daughter, stealing an important connection.

Josh thought over his options. He had to say something, but the only thing he could think of meant revealing his secret side, which Evander surely wouldn't appreciate or admire. But that wasn't why Josh was here, was it? He had come to deliver a ring so the man could ask the woman of his life to be with him forever, not to earn the man's approval. And anyway, Tigger would rat him out soon enough with her joy over his creations.

"It's stuff I make for the Children's Burn Unit in Toronto," Josh said quickly. "Hair accessories, fairy art. It..." He tried to find words to express what he did without sounding too effeminate to the former marine.

Evander cleared his throat. "Fairies?"

"Yeah. Fairies," Josh admitted reluctantly.

"Oh, thank God." Evander stood, clapping him on the shoulder. "You don't know what a relief it is to hear that."

Josh blinked in surprise. That really wasn't the reaction he'd been expecting, but now he wondered which avenue Evander's assumptions were traveling down.

"It's very girlie stuff, but I'm not, uh..."

"That's perfect. Great." Evander tossed up his hands. "You don't know how happy this makes me."

"I'm not gay."

Evander was suddenly on guard. "What does that mean?"

"Just because I enjoy making pink, lacy, sequined hair accessories and fairy art doesn't mean I'm gay." There. He'd said it. Out loud.

He'd admitted he was different, despite the possible consequences. Simone had gone forth in the fashion world and prospered; so could he.

Josh squared his shoulders, ready to take the first fist. It was going to hurt like hell, but maybe his snowsuit would help cushion the blow if Evander hit him in the gut.

"What's wrong with being gay?" the big man asked, eyes narrowed.

"Nothing." Josh should loosen the muscles in his jaw so it wouldn't snap. He reminded himself not to tense, to allow himself to get tossed aside, go with the impact, not resist it.

"What are you saying?"

"Nothing." *Jaw loose.* "I'm not gay. I like women." He shook the tension out of his hands.

"Daphne is mine and you'd better stay the hell away from Tigger!" the man roared.

Josh blocked his face in anticipation, but Evander didn't strike.

"Are you homophobic?" The bodyguard was close, his breathing harsh and loud through his clenched teeth. He was studying him with a glint in his eye that Josh sure didn't like. It was protective and fierce, which meant he'd fight like a mad fool, out to destroy anything he perceived as a threat. "Because my brother is gay and I've seen the shit he's had to deal with, so you'd better watch your mouth or I'll—"

"My dad is transgender," Josh blurted out, wincing as the words hit their mark, his hands still held protectively in front of his face. Christ. He was going all-out tonight, wasn't he?

Evander's fist dropped, but the defensive challenge still laced his voice. "So?"

"So I know all about the stuff your brother faces and the fights he gets into because of his sexuality. He wouldn't choose that kind of social rejection if he had a choice. Nobody would." *Except me, now that I'm coming out with my creations.* Man, he was nuts. "And he's incredibly brave to follow the beat of his own internal drum. It's more than most people can do."

"Then why are you making a big deal out of homosexuality?"

"Have you ever seen a man who wasn't gay create pink frilly things for little girls and find it incredibly rewarding? How do you think that goes over? Usually 'different' means getting a fist in your gut."

Evander laughed and slapped Josh on the back, his face lit up with amusement. "If I hadn't seen that hungry look in your eye whenever you spy Simone I'd think you were gay based solely on that."

"What hungry look?"

Evander simply gave him a smile and Josh let out an

aggravated sigh, then flicked the generator switch. To his surprise, the engine roared to life. It looked as though the machine had merely overheated.

Evander stomped the snow off his boots outside the cottage door, then opened it, hollering, "Guess who fixed the generator? Someone had better show Josh some love under the mistletoe."

He winked at him, then disappeared inside.

Josh hesitated, wondering why his heart had lifted at the thought of the beautiful and difficult Simone rewarding him under the mistletoe.

JOSH LET HIMSELF WARM UP in front of the fire before peeling off his snowsuit. The temperature had dropped outside over the past hour and a half and the wind was definitely too much for a helicopter, even though the flakes were no longer piling up in the same way.

"That storm is not letting up," Connor said to the group.

"Are we here for the night?" Simone asked. Her arms were crossed under her breasts, lifting and pushing in a way Josh would love to see without the hindrance of her sweater and undergarments. Which made him realize that the men had been right—he'd developed a hunger for her. However, that didn't mean it was going to go any further than that. She was prickly and didn't want to let anyone close even though she kissed like an angel. A steamy, sexy angel who moved her mouth in erotic ways that were going to cause a commotion in his pants if he didn't distract himself.

Distraction, distraction...well, he could just ponder how judgmental she was. That would surely make any man flaccid. She was so damned determined. She hadn't even asked for her friends' support with her whole baby thing. Talk about a powerhouse holding her cards close. She didn't just have walls, she had a moat, fire-breathing dragons, molten lava, and burning oil ready to take down anyone who dared think of lending her sympathy or support.

What the hell kind of past had made her like that?

"We're spending the night?" Hailey asked with a yawn.

"Looks that way," Finian replied, massaging her shoulders.

"It'll probably clear up by morning," Tristen offered.

"I hope so," Simone grumbled.

"Better find someone warm and cozy up," Connor said, aiming a sly grin at Josh.

Cozy up. His eyes drifted to Simone, who met his gaze with a glare. He tried to fight a smile, but it broke through anyway, defying his wishes.

"Come on, baby." He held out his arms to her. "You know you want it," he teased. "You know you want a real man to hold you at night."

She made a disgusted sound in the back of her throat and turned on her heel. "Come on, Tigger. Let's set you up with a bed."

"I'm writing a letter to Santa with Evander. We're not done yet." She waved the half-written page as evidence.

Tristen's daughter, Dot, who had been dozing in the window seat, said, "Is it warm upstairs yet?"

"Let's check," her father replied.

"Sleepover with Dot!" Tigger said, bouncing up, her letter forgotten.

Tristen and Evander moved up the stairs that led to a loft, to ensure the heater they'd set up was doing its job.

"Come on, Tigger," Evander said. "Let's get you settled. You'll have to sleep in your clothes tonight."

"Will Santa still come if we stay here?" Tigger called up the steps, not following.

Evander's head appeared. "I don't think Santa knows you're staying here tonight."

Tigger gave him a worried look and Josh stepped in, hoping Evander would be okay with his interference. "When I was a kid, Santa always left gifts for me at home even when we got snowed in at my grandma's once. He won't forget you."

Noticing that she still had his phone, he held out his hand for it. The girl reluctantly placed it in his palm. "I organized it by colors." She pointed at the folders she had created. Sure enough, all the blue apps were in one folder, all the orange ones in another. He wondered what else she had done while he hadn't been paying attention.

"That's great, thanks."

"First ride out," Connor said softly to Evander, who had come back down the stairs for Tigger. The men shared a look, everyone silently agreeing that they'd work as a team to get either Evander or Daphne home before the little girl, so Santa could prepare for her arrival.

People shuffled up and down the stairs, arranging beds, gathering extra bedding from upstairs and preparing the group for the night. Josh stayed out of the way, assuming he'd tough it out in front of the fire. Keep it going. Listen for the generator. Keep an eye out for the miraculous return of cell service or a rescue party. It wouldn't be the first time he'd stayed up all night with nothing but flames for company. His attention still snapped to it whenever a log popped, but so far he'd resisted the urge to check the smoke detectors. He had a pretty good feeling they were outdated or had dead batteries, and that there were nowhere near enough in this old building to meet code. In fact, the one outside the kitchen door was hanging from its wiring.

He tried to make himself not care, but finally gave in and grabbed a chair, stepping up on it so he could test the dangling smoke detector.

It bleated shrilly in his ear. It worked and he was now deaf. He tucked the device back into its mounting bracket.

"Oh, don't do that," Melanie said. "We can't pull the battery out when we burn toast otherwise."

Pull the battery out. She'd just said that. A lawyer. A woman with more degrees than he could shake a stick at pulled the batteries out of smoke detectors. The very device that could save her life on a night like this.

"I'm a firefighter," he said, summoning patience. "I can't stay in a building where the smoke detector isn't functioning in the way it was designed to. And it was designed to be in its brace. Once I'm gone, go ahead and do what you want, but I really need this in place tonight."

Melanie shrugged. "Okay. That's fine. I get where you're coming from."

If only Simone was as accommodating as her friend.

"And how's that fire extinguisher?" He pointed to the red metal canister peeking out from under a pile of old rags near the kitchen door. "Has it expired?"

"They expire?"

Grant him serenity.

"Their neck seal weakens and they lose pressure. Especially if they've been discharged at all."

"Oh."

Great. He was going to be pulling people from a burning building in the middle of the night, wasn't he?

"Thanks for fixing that," Melanie said as he returned the chair to the card table, having righted the fire extinguisher and giving it a tap on its bottom in hopes of loosening its contents. "You went to Camp Adaker, didn't you?" she added, joining him near what was becoming his favorite chair in front of the fire.

Josh felt himself bristle. Not where he expected the conversation to go. "This place is old and dry. You need to be careful with fire here."

"You don't want to talk about it?" she asked gently.

Adaker had been a summer camp for troubled teens. Some kids went there for a week. Some, like him, came for several summers before they figured out the light of day wasn't out to get them.

He sighed. "It's okay. The camp was good."

"I liked it."

"You went there?" he asked, not masking his surprise.

She nodded. "Shortly after my dad died. I thought I was the only person who'd had anything bad happened to them. The camp helped."

Yeah, seeing kids who were truly up crap creek would have helped. Perspective and all that. He'd finally realized in year two that his problems really weren't that bad. Nobody was beating him unconscious at the dinner table for not passing the salt fast enough, like some of those kids.

"Polly said they closed the camp?"

"They did, but these guys—" she jerked a thumb over her shoulder "—went and bought the whole darn island. Including the camp." She gave a soft smile. "I'm going to open it again next summer. My grandma was one of the camp's founders."

"Keeping it in the family."

She smiled, her eyes so warm and open that Josh felt himself relax. "Good luck. It provides a good service."

"Thank you. I was wondering though...did the camp help you? Truly?"

"Yeah." He glanced around, feeling self-conscious. He didn't really want to talk about the camp with Simone around. He was a different person than he'd been back then, young and confused, controlled by a pulsing need to beat the snot out of anyone who stood in the way of his father's happiness. If Simone heard he'd been at Adaker she'd go on about the macho thing again, either that or think he was a wimp who couldn't handle his feelings and was in need of saving. Neither shoe fit.

Melanie lowered her voice. "Could I ask you about it one day? Nothing too personal. Just what helped and what didn't? When I reopen the camp I want to take things up a notch. Not that it wasn't great, but I want to have a good sense of what worked and what didn't. You know? So I don't cut the good stuff."

"Yeah. Sure." He pushed his hands into his thighs, stretching out his back. "That would be fine." He glanced around the room. "Just...just make sure you keep the hands-on social workers. They were amazing."

Melanie pressed a palm to his knee as he cleared his throat twice, trying to dislodge the lump that had formed.

He stood, poking at the fire even though it didn't need it. He glanced up and said quickly, "Thanks for keeping Adaker open."

She leaned back in the chair, clearly happy. "My grandma and her lover started the camp decades ago. Can't let it go now, right?"

"Could I have everyone's attention, please?" It was Evander. His tone was take-charge and everyone turned to face him. He coughed, fist to his mouth, then reached for Daphne, pulling her close. "Some amazing things happened last summer. To all of us." He gave an apologetic look to Simone, and Josh wondered what was going on. "I've met royalty and worked in some amazing parts of the world, but the most incredible thing to ever happen has been Daphne allowing me to be a part of her life."

"Me, too?" asked Tigger hopefully.

"You, too." He ruffled her curls and she beamed up at him with so much love that Josh wished he could escape the private moment that was unfurling around him.

Evander cleared his throat. "With one look, Daphne breathed new hope and light into my heart. I had believed I was broken beyond repair, but I wasn't. I just needed the love of this amazing woman, and I'm grateful for her every single day. I am blessed she gave me a chance."

He glanced at Tigger and added, "And you, too, Miss Bounce."

The girl beamed from her seat beside him, bouncing on her hands, which were tucked under her dress.

"I'm not always good with words, but I think it suffices to say that Daphne was right when she told me love changes the world. It starts with one person and spreads from there. And so I will do whatever I can to help her spread love. I will do whatever I need to ensure Daphne and her daughter are always happy, always safe and always loved. I know that Mr. Summer passed away a long time ago and Catherine not so long ago." He cleared his throat again. "So, as I stand before you all, I summon your blessings as Daphne's family as I ask for her hand in marriage."

He lowered himself to one knee, drawing a small engagement ring from his back pocket. He held it out for Daphne, who bit her lip, trying to contain the joy that was already making her small frame vibrate. "Daphne, will you complete my life, my happiness, my heart, and marry me?"

"Say yes!" Tigger squealed, so loudly Josh laughed and rubbed his ears.

Daphne was silent for a long moment, looking so somber Josh feared she was going to refuse. Then she whispered, "I'm pregnant."

The room was deathly quiet, then Evander stood slowly, looking enormous.

"We're having a baby, Evander."

"A baby!" Tigger nearly fell over. She pretended to fan herself, then jumped up and down, her little-girl persona breaking through her attempt at ladylike drama. "Make it a *sister!*"

Evander swept up Daphne, holding her close, not speaking. Muffled choking sounds came from the man, then he whooped loudly and swung her in circles, bouncing as he went, nearly knocking over nearby chairs, the floor creaking with his weight as he laughed with joy. He set his girlfriend down again, his eyes red-rimmed, his expression suddenly so somber, his mouth shaking with emotion. Then he crushed her against him once more, breathing her in.

"Uh, did we get an answer?" Dot asked.

Evander pushed Daphne away, clinging tight to her arms. He was pale, serious, ring still clutched between his large fingers.

She simply smiled up at him before blinking back tears and nodding, mouthing the word *yes*. She nodded again, more vigorously. "Yes!" She fell into his arms and he wrapped himself around her so completely that everyone clapped and cheered. A happy ending for a man who had only moments ago been completely insecure about the worth of his love.

"Yay!" Tigger piled onto the couple. "Evander's my forever daddy and I'm going to be a sister!"

Josh glanced around the room. The other Summers were all smiling, embracing their own men, happy for their youngest sibling as Evander slipped a ring on her fingers.

And yet Simone was ghostly white, rocking back and forth as though preparing to start a race. She glanced up at the snowshoes above the fireplace and Josh knew he was going to have to keep an eye on her. Something was going on inside her head and it wasn't good.

Chapter Seven

As Daphne and Evander kissed each other as fiancée and fiancé, Simone found herself glancing over at JC to ensure their deal was still on. He gave a small nod, looking as serious and determined as she felt.

She no longer belonged here. Everyone was happy. Everyone was hooking up, having babies and moving on with their lives. She was moving on, too, in terms of her livelihood and identity, but it was all so incredibly fast. Everything was changing. Simone was no longer like her friends. Daphne had a family and was now making it official. Hailey was starting one, and the way Maya kept joking about puking, she was likely along the way, too. Even the proper do-it-by-the-book Melanie was trying to get pregnant before her wedding.

Simone didn't even want to think about what was happening in her father's life.

Everyone was getting what they wanted. Everyone was expanding their love, happiness radiating outward in waves, new people popping up on the planet as a result, and it made her desperate to have someone who would love her back.

Simone pulled out her sketchpad to clear her mind, despite having promised herself to ignore fresh ideas so they wouldn't take over her new life. She leaned her shoulder against the mantel and, after taking a cleansing breath, used Maya as inspiration for her design. Around the room, adults still fussed over bedding and sleeping arrangements, as well as Daphne's news.

With quick strokes of her pencil, Simone found herself digging into her own past instead of creating something for her friend.

Wanda's words from the latest MOM meeting echoed in her mind. *There's nothing I can stock in my boutique that works for the twelve to seventeen-year-old crowd. It's either too provocative, too little girlish or too mature. That age group is like the black hole of formal wear. Don't even get me started on larger-sized gowns.*

And didn't Simone know it.

Memories of junior prom gowns flashed through her mind. Lots and lots of prom gowns, but only a handful that fit. Feelings of inadequacy, of being fat, uncomfortable, unattractive and different in all the wrong ways washed over her as though she was still in the moment, trying on dresses with Hailey. While her friend had been complaining that she'd have to take in the waists on many of the trendy garments, Simone had been wondering how she could make the adult-sized dresses into something hip and less revealing.

Every garment she tried on had been a shock to her system, sending her into a month-long depression that had been just as bad as when her parents had split a few months prior. The trauma caused her to pile on even more weight, adding to her prom dress problem. Her feelings of inadequacy had underscored everything as though drawn with a heavy hand in charcoal, and it wasn't until she began designing gowns like the one coming to life on her sketchpad that she'd come back around again.

Simone held out her pad and studied it critically. She'd come full circle, hadn't she? Starting with plus-sized gowns and ending with them.

Or maybe it wasn't full circle, maybe it was just a new start. The right start. The path she was actually supposed to follow. It was possible she'd sold her old brand, kit and caboodle, for a reason and now she could follow this new path without the restrictions or hesitation that came with an established brand name.

JC moved closer, reaching out to touch her shoulder. She shifted away, afraid the sweet gesture would make her insecurities rear up, ready for attack. But instead of making contact, he braced himself against the mantel, so smoothly she doubted he'd actually intended to touch her.

"Nice. Very goddess-like." He was more curious and appraising than judgmental as he looked over her shoulder.

She pulled the screen away from the fireplace and tossed the sketchpad inside.

No new beginnings. They took too much time and would take her away from her dreams of a family. She was shifting back to her comfort zone and that needed to stop.

"Why'd you do that?" he asked, scrambling for the poker so he could fish out the smoking pad. "It was good!"

"Leave it." Flames licked the edges of the pages. "I'm not starting any new projects."

"You're hard-core, woman." He kneaded her shoulder and she let out a breathy laugh, not quite believing she'd tossed half a year's worth of designs in the fire.

"Oh, God! Get it out!" She pulled the poker out of JC's grip as the papers ignited, sending out a flash of heat. "Those were good ideas."

"They'll be even better the second time you sketch them. More refined."

"How do you know?" She turned to watch him, curious.

JC gave a nonchalant shrug. "Still snowing out there?"

His walls had been raised and Simone decided not to pursue it.

"Not exactly how you anticipated spending your Christmas

Eve, huh?" She refused to move away, even though he had placed himself squarely in her space as though she needed support. "Stuck here. Will Polly and your family be worried?"

"Probably." He looked at her with a steady gaze. Why wasn't he freaking out about his family worrying? Oh, right. Because he was one of those men who expected the world to revolve around him, and any problems were always someone else's. Machismo. She kept forgetting that. Especially when she met his kind eyes, which often flashed with secrets and pain.

"Is anyone else expecting you?" Simone hated herself for holding her breath as she waited for his reply, but a part of her needed to know. She knew he wasn't married, but he was a handsome man who fought fires for a living. He probably had twenty women waiting for him to call tonight.

That idea shouldn't bother her nearly as much as it did.

Except he'd kissed her. Repeatedly. And it had been better and better each time.

"A girlfriend?" JC asked, eyebrow lifted as though he thought he might be winning some sort of game. "Need someone to cozy up to, and you're worried about infringing on someone else's property?"

"No, just wondering who I need to apologize to once you find my charms irresistible."

JC choked on a chuckle and Simone turned away, pleased by her quick retort.

"Connor?" She waited for him to stop nuzzling Maya's ear and pay attention. "Don't you have sled dogs at your disposal? Emergency helicopters that are used to flying in Antarctica where there are blizzards all the time? This guy's got people panicking that he's vanished off the face of the earth, and while he obviously doesn't care about it, I think we should make an effort to get him off the island."

"You're voting me off?" JC said, his voice quiet behind her, sending chills up her spine. She could take a half step back and be in his arms, her body pressed against his rock-hard form.

"There is no vote." She prompted Connor, "So? Don't you?"

Everyone was staring at her. "What?" she asked.

"If my people felt they could get here safely, they would be here," Connor replied. "We're okay where we are for the next while, so let's focus on the joy of being disconnected from the world. Let's celebrate being together with family and friends."

"Well, I guess I'll take one of the extra beds upstairs?" she said. The fact that nobody had mentioned where she'd be sleeping was starting to feel a bit suspicious, and she was beginning to suspect that she was going to end up toughing it out with JC in front of the fire.

Maya gave Connor a swift glance.

"What?" Simone asked.

"We, um, kind of took them out when we were perking up the décor this summer. There are two cots up there. Maybe Tigger could sleep on the couch instead of with Dot?"

Since the marriage proposal the girl had received a second wind, and had been tucked away in the corner, furiously dictating the rest of her letter to Santa via Evander.

"I'm sleeping with Dot!" Tigger announced, bottom lip thrust out. "Upstairs!"

Simone threw up her hands, knowing better than to fight with the little girl when she stuck out her bottom lip. "Fine," Simone said. "I can sleep on the couch."

Which meant JC was going to sleep where? In a chair?

"Unless you want the couch," she offered grudgingly. He gave her a dark, unimpressed look.

"Okay, it's mine then. Thank you." She primly turned away,

trying hard not to think about how close she would be sleeping to him.

"Well, I'm calling it a night," Hailey said, stretching her arms above her head. "Growing a baby makes me tired." She shot Simone an apologetic look.

"Of course. You need to take care of yourself," Simone said. She wrapped her arms around herself. "Do we have enough firewood to get us through the night?"

"I carried some in earlier," Finian said.

"And I cleared the roof," Evander added. "The snow load should be okay through this storm."

Great. Another thing to worry about: the roof falling in on them due to the weight of the snow Mother Nature was using to bury them alive.

JC was pulling on his snowsuit, zipping it up, the bulky outerwear covering his well-defined chest. "Where's the woodpile?"

Finian went out with him and Simone relaxed, fidgeting with the burn holes in her jeans. As much as she hated to admit it, she trusted JC to take care of things. As Hailey had said earlier, he was a fixer, too. Or rescuer. Whatever. Same difference. But it was starting to feel as though she was relying on him too much for basic survival. She wanted to wade through the snow to get more wood, too, if only to prove that she didn't need him.

"Are you okay?" Hailey asked, head cocked to the side.

"Fine. Great. Just, you know, problem solving." She caught Tigger as the girl bounced past, her letter finished. "Let's get you into that bed, kiddo. I'll tell you a story, how's that sound?"

"Are you sleeping with Uncle Josh tonight?" Tigger asked, her eyes so full of innocence and hope.

Simone needed someone who would think she was enough, no matter what she did or didn't do with her life, and the men like JC she'd dated always wanted her to change, always wanted more. They always wanted that "something" she didn't seem to possess.

She took a deep breath before replying. "He isn't my type, sweetie."

"You should make him your type."

Yeah, that's what her body kept telling her, too.

SIMONE HAD JUST FINISHED telling a story to Tigger—and Dot, who had pretended not to listen on the neighboring cot, but hadn't turned a single page in her book the entire time—when she heard JC's voice downstairs. She let out a sigh of relief, knowing they likely now had enough wood to get them through the night, plus some. The man would make a good provider and protector for someone who liked that sort of thing.

"Josh!" Tigger hollered from beside Simone, startling her.

Heavy feet pounded up the wood steps to the attic and Josh called, "Yeah?"

"Come up here."

Simone stayed where she was on the cot, curious about what Tigger was up to.

"We're friends, right?" the little girl asked, when his head poked over the railing.

"Yup," he said simply. He moved to the top step, hand gripping the banister. His cheeks were bright red from darting out into the cold night, his shoulders as broad as ever. He looked handsome and strong, intent on making sure Tigger knew she was important and heard. Not all adults took the time to do that, and while that quality had always softened Simone, she hadn't expected it in a man such as JC, and for some reason it made her angry. The man was supposed to stay in his arrogant little box, not mess with her mind by being caring and great with kids.

He was being a heart slayer, which was completely unfair.

"Friends get friends Christmas presents, right?" Tigger questioned. Simone chuckled, scolding her gently for being so forward.

"Of course they do," Josh replied.

The girl beckoned him over, sitting up. Only a moment ago Simone had her close to falling asleep, but now she was as wide awake as Dot.

"Phone." Tigger held out her hand expectantly.

Josh passed it to her and she punched in his access code.

"Wait. You know his code?" Simone asked.

"I changed it to my birthday," the girl said, zipping through the contents, her mind on one thing.

Josh laughed. "Were you planning to tell me that or leave me locked out of my phone forever?"

"Forever."

Simone bit her bottom lip, trying not to laugh, and Josh shook his head, his eyes crinkling with amusement.

"Never give a kid your phone," Dot said from her cot. "First rule of ownership."

"Too bad this bright adult male didn't think of that," Simone teased.

JC sat beside her on Tigger's small bed, too close for comfort, but Simone forced herself to stay, to stand her ground even though the heat coming off him felt too familiar, too consuming. It reminded her of how irresistible he was when she let her guard down. But he wasn't her type. The two of them were opposites, or too much alike, too something. Something that would make them fight all the time and weaken the very defenses she needed in order to survive.

She sighed, knowing a man such as JC could throw her off

track, and she had too much at stake. And yet...and yet he tempted her much more than she cared to admit.

"This." Tigger held up JC's phone. "I want this."

"In pink?" JC replied. "Or purple?"

"Purple so it matches the dress Simone is making me. She makes me lots of dresses. Can you tuck me in?"

Simone snatched the phone, holding it still so she could get a better look at the photo of an adorable frilly doodad. "You have Internet connection? When did you get a link? We need to call the helicopters."

"They're pictures," Tigger said, suddenly sleepy again.

"From the Internet, which means he has signal."

"Maybe he could have a show in your boutique like Mom and Hailey did. Mom sold lots of paintings."

Simone ignored the girl while she searched for the phone app. "Why do you have all of your apps arranged by color?" The man was proving to be more and more nutters. Definitely not good dad material.

She dialed 911. Nothing but silence as she held the phone to her ear. She checked the cell signal. No bars of service. What on earth?

"Slow down," JC said, laying a hand over hers, then taking his phone back. His palm was large, warm, and oddly comforting. And made her mind flash to other things besides getting off this island. "They're photos of things I make for kids."

She tried to look at his phone again, but he had turned it off, slipping it into his faded jeans pocket. And now she was staring at his crotch's bulge.

Man, these hormones were getting out of control.

"He makes really pretty hair ribbons and barrettes."

JC was calm, his voice low and soothing. "I make them for kids in the burn unit."

Simone felt as though she was lost in a funhouse. Only it wasn't fun. The hair ribbons she'd seen had been delicate, beautiful, well-crafted, and unique. She'd barely had a glance at them, but knew they were special and that the creator had talent.

How could JC create something like that?

It was impossible. The man jumped out of airplanes so he could face off against raging forest fires. He got into fistfights and was built like a steamy, sexy hunk of manhood. Creating delicate girlie things by hand was not manly. It was not JC.

It made no sense. It didn't add up.

"I've been thinking about expanding my own little business. I was hoping you and I could talk about distribution if you have time."

Simone sat up, jostling Tigger in the process. "Get the creator to call me and we'll set something up, but I'm not dealing with a middleman." Her heart was pounding like mad as she felt her world slipping. "I deal with the heart of the business—the creator. And tell her that candy-apple red is too overstated. Even for a child."

Dot, who had been watching the exchange, quietly slipped away, scurrying like a cat in a roomful of guard dogs.

Josh paused for a second, then gave a slight, thoughtful nod.

"He is the heart," Tigger said, her voice laced with confusion.

"Him?" Simone shook her head. "Tigger, no. Not possible."

"He makes fairy art, too."

"No, he doesn't."

"I'll show you!" The girl hopped up and trundled down the stairs. "Wait here."

Fairy art? The man was so freaking manly he was stirring up parts of Simone that had been on life support for years. He couldn't be gay. It wouldn't be fair to womankind.

No, it didn't matter. She knew who he was and she didn't want him. Let him be gay. That would be a relief, actually. It would make him a lot less dangerous and make a lot more sense.

"So you're a gay man masquerading as some big macho alpha dude?" Simone laughed, relief washing over her like a downpour after years of drought. She clapped her hands as she stood. "That's *so* perfect."

He scowled up at her and she placed her palms on either side of his cheeks in joy. Who cared if he was angry that she'd figured out his secret? She'd known there was no way the old JC could make something so delicately beautiful. She'd *known* something was up with him. Known he wasn't real—because he was a fake.

She placed her lips on his, kissing him with happiness and relief. He was gay! She was safe!

His fingers knotted in her hair, drawing her close. Her eyes flew open as his kiss turned angry and possessive. And hot. Really freaking hot. It was as though he was trying to prove something to her and...wow. It was as though a bell was being rung again and again as his mouth worked hers in angry, hungry passes.

He pulled her into his lap, their surroundings forgotten. She straddled him, lost in the kiss and the way her body was begging for all he could give her. This was the best kiss she'd ever had, point-blank. It was passionate and barely contained. Her control was slipping and she didn't care.

His hand moved up to her breast, caressing her, and she involuntarily ground her pelvis against him. She jumped back when she rubbed something very hard. She fell out of his arms, landing on the floor.

Gay men didn't get stiff kissing women.

Oh, no, JC wasn't gay. Gay men didn't consume women in passionate kisses.

He was as straight as a prairie highway.

What had she been doing? Where was her mind?

"What the hell?" she barked.

He stood up, his mouth set in that angry way of his that made her want to take him down a notch for being so...so JC.

"You are *such* a liar!"

"What are you talking about?" He scowled.

"Are you gay or not gay?"

"What does that matter? You're not open-minded enough to see that I'm the best thing that could ever happen to you."

"Best thing?" She snorted and focused on his chest, which was rising and falling as quickly as hers. "You're a big hoax. A liar. A façade. A bunch of false advertising in a big sexy body. You're a—a..." Words failed her as she looked up into his eyes. His anger was gone and had been replaced with resignation and disappointment. In her.

No. Nobody was *ever* disappointed in her. She *exceeded* expectations. That's what she did. That was her *thing*.

He pulled her up off the floor, gently rubbing his thumb over her knuckles before letting her go.

"I hope you find what you're looking for, Simone."

He gave her one last glance before heading down the stairs, pausing to murmur something to a returning Tigger as Simone sank onto the vacated cot, feeling as though she might cry, her heart slashed by a sense of devastating loss.

SIMONE WAS GETTING UNDER Josh's skin. She'd been so hot and cold. Strong and vulnerable. Push and pull. Tease and withdraw. And then the gay comment? It was as if a rocket had gone off in his brain. When she'd bent down to give him that patronizing "you're gay so I'm saved from being attracted to you" kiss, it had been all he could do to keep from proving just how hetero he was.

The worst part was that she had been right. The candy-apple red was overstated. It wasn't a big deal, but her offhand comment showed him just how out of his depth he'd swum. She had an instinctual color sense he lacked. He'd been working on trying to develop it and had barely branched out from pink, knowing it was beyond his current skills. And she'd taken one glimpse and known.

Over. His. Head.

He couldn't do this, could he? He was going to fail and look like a dumbass. There was a reason men didn't do this kind of stuff.

They did other things. Manly things that didn't get them called gay.

And dammit. He knew he wasn't a homosexual, so why did that term still get a rise out of him? Wasn't he beyond that by now?

But Simone. Man. JC pushed his fingers through his hair and stood on the back porch of the cottage, hoping to freeze away the heat that lingered from their do-me kiss. He could still feel the lushness of her breast, the potent response of his body and how it had demanded to prove his virility.

Thinking about her was not helping, but it did distract him from the self-loathing that was flaring up like a beast.

Despite the fact that it was cold enough out to prevent most gas-powered vehicles from starting, he was still growing an erection so big he could use it as a flagpole. He was going to have the worst case of blue balls. And from what? One kiss with a woman who hated him. But the way she'd come alive, the way all her prickly barriers had come crashing down as she'd gotten into their session... There was none of that "must protect myself from

Josh at all costs" thing she normally had going on. She'd gotten into it. Gotten hot. Really hot.

He'd liked it.

A lot.

He wanted to kiss her again.

And then some more.

A lot more.

The door behind him creaked open.

"How's the weather?"

It was Connor, shoulders hunched under his thick sweater.

"Better than it was." It wasn't howling as it had been an hour ago, but still beyond anything a helicopter could get through, or a safety-conscious snowmobiler would try to tackle.

"And how are things inside?"

Josh shrugged, pretending he didn't understand where Connor was heading.

"Making any progress?"

"How so?"

"It's none of my business, but I figured there were only three reasons a man would come stand out in a blizzard without a jacket, and seeing as you aren't a smoker, that leaves us with either you want off this island bad enough to risk your own life so you can get away from her, or she's got you so fired up you need to cool your jets."

Josh chuckled. The man had him pegged, all right.

Connor gave him a light punch in the arm. "She might be standoffish and difficult, but she's worth it if she's already got you feeling like this after a few hours of being stuck with her." He leaned closer, as though someone might overhear. "And when you do get together, all that spitfire attitude..." He grinned and shook his head. "You'd better watch out. It'll be like no other woman you've ever experienced. Trust me." He held the door open behind him. Considering the rest of his body was feeling as blue from the cold as his balls were going to be come morning, Josh followed the man inside.

The warm scent of old wood paneling met them as Connor walked ahead, passing through the chilly kitchen and into the living room, arms stretched high as he yawned loudly. "Well, I'm calling it a night. Let's hope the heat keeps working or we'll all be cuddling with Josh and Simone tonight."

Connor gave his wife a look that said all sorts of naughty things, and the couple, giggling, vanished from the room.

Simone was staring into the fire, fingers pressed to her lips, shutting out the world. Josh liked to think that maybe he'd gotten under her skin, as well.

Daphne, who had finally managed to get Tigger settled, headed off for the night with Evander, while Melanie and Tristen lingered to see if Simone and Josh had all they needed. Judging by the stack of blankets and pillows, as well as the pile of firewood, Josh deemed them set.

"So?" he said to Simone as he shook out a blanket, folding it around himself as he took the chair opposite her. He crushed a pillow behind his head and leaned back, kicking out his feet. He was still pissed at how she'd discounted his hair accessories, denying the possibility that he'd be capable of creating something delicate.

She ignored him.

He shut his eyes, making himself comfortable. Tomorrow she'd be out of his hair. Tomorrow, tomorrow. Then he could go find someone in a bar for a one-night stand, and shake Simone out of his system.

He shifted in the chair, unable to get comfortable, the pillow pressing against the tender bump on his head.

Straight men could create pretty things. They could bring joy into the world in ways other than saving cats from burning barns.

But Simone had said she wanted to talk to the creator. That had to mean she liked them, and saw potential, right?

That he was rocking it.

He opened one eye. "Still think I'm gay?"

She whirled, glaring at him. "I don't appreciate you playing games with me." Her voice was low, so as not to bother the others through the thin cottage walls.

"No games. This is me."

"You don't add up."

"Because you have an outdated calculator that's as narrow-minded as you are," he snapped, whipping the blanket off his legs.

"I am not narrow-minded."

"Prove it."

She blinked, chin tipped down.

"Stop assuming I'm either a pushy, overbearing jerk who wants to run your life or that I'm gay and living a lie."

"You are a liar."

If you denied your true self long enough, did that make you a liar?

"See? You're not denying it." She smirked as though she'd won a point. But instead of being bothered, he found himself wanting to break down her barriers more than ever. All that attitude, all that fire. They could have a lot of fun if she let him in.

He moved to her swiftly, pulling her out of her chair and into an embrace. "And you're a liar by denying how much chemistry we have going on between us, and the fact that it scares you."

She pushed lightly on his chest, a feeble halfhearted move that told him she wanted to stay exactly where she was, wrapped in his arms. "You don't scare me."

"Right."

"Why would I be afraid of you?"

She was looking up at him with dark, curious eyes.

"You tell me." He lowered his lips to hers, and was rewarded with that surge of desire sparking to life inside him—same as always. This time it was less out of control, but just as hot and needy. He swept his thumb over her hollowed cheek as she deepened the kiss. Cupping her below the waist, he pulled her body to his.

She broke away, eyelids at half-mast. "We're not good for each other."

"I think we are."

"No."

He dropped his arms, already wanting to hold her again. "Do you always deny everything that's right in your life?"

Her body turned rigid as anger flared. "And are you so cocky to think you could actually offer me what I need?"

"What do you need, Simone?" He fought a growing resentment for her brick walls and tried to soften his attitude so he wouldn't act like the man she thought he was.

"I need a man who's not you." Her voice was wobbly, her eyes blinking furiously.

He had a hold on her, but somewhere in her life she'd become so shaken that he wondered what it would take for her to cross the barrier that kept her at bay. Whatever it was, he found himself that much more determined to have her, to win her over.

Simone Pascal was going to be his by the time they said goodbye.

Chapter Eight

Josh had been sleeping lightly, waking every hour or so to place more logs on the fire so Simone wouldn't have to. Each time, he'd taken a moment to watch her sleep, wondering what had her so spooked and how he could circumvent it. She'd become an irresistible challenge, a mystery to crack. But so far he'd gathered no hints other than what he already knew about her. She was strong. Clever. Independent and allusive. Keeping secrets from her friends just as he did.

Had she been burned one too many times? Or was she just fiercely independent to a fault?

The fire was still going strong, and before drifting off again, he glanced over to check on Simone, who was sleeping on the couch just behind him. Her blankets were crumpled, her supple form no longer denting the cushions. He sat up straighter, listening for her. All was quiet other than the fire and gentle background hum of the generator and bedroom heaters.

He checked his phone. It was 4:00 a.m. He'd last been up at two. How had he managed to sleep through Simone stoking the fire?

He rubbed his eyes and got up to check the common areas, tenderly exploring the bump on his head, which had shrunk considerably. Simone wasn't in the kitchen, nor the nonfunctioning bathroom. There was still plenty of firewood.

Had she gone to the outhouse?

He checked the time again. How long had she been outside? Was she properly dressed? Was she even out there? Maybe she was comforting Tigger, who'd had a bad dream or something.

No. The snowshoes that hung above the fireplace were gone and, when he checked, the mat at the door was short one pair of women's boots.

She was outdoors. On snowshoes.

Heading home? He didn't think so. That seemed too fraught with risk for even the determined and obsessively independent Simone.

You couldn't have a baby if you were frozen in a snowdrift. So where did she go? And why?

Had to be the outhouse.

Josh hurried to put on his suit and boots, hoping to bump into her as she came in from the cold, but still he prepared for the worst. Gathering lights and a blanket, he opened the back door off the kitchen, disappointed and alarmed when he didn't find her standing there.

"Simone?" he called, not caring if he woke anyone. There was no reply but the haunting sound of grainy snow scurrying over hard, crusted drifts.

"Damn independent woman," he muttered under his breath as he clipped the spare flashlight onto the back clothesline. She should know better than to go out alone. She should have woken him up, told him where she was heading.

He kicked himself for sleeping through her departure, and scanned for telltale tracks in the snow. His earlier path to the woodpile had drifted over, obliterated by shifting snow. But a large set of indentations led toward the outhouse. Snowshoes.

He swung his light out into the darkness, calling Simone once again before setting off.

Finally, near the outhouse, he heard a reply to his frequent calls. "Here! I'm here! JC?"

JC? Nobody had called him that since he was a teenager. Which meant she likely assumed he was the same troublemaking goof from back then. He still was in some ways, but he liked to think he'd changed at least a little bit and had allowed his finer traits to develop as he matured.

"Simone?" He cast the light over the snow, wondering if the wind was playing tricks with his ears.

Out of the corner of his eye he caught sight of a feeble band of light shining up into an evergreen. Josh hurried through the dark night, the flying flakes dizzying as he swung the light, searching for her.

"Simone?"

"JC!"

She was scrambling like a wounded bird, stuck under the branches of a spruce. The wind had created a deep bowl around the tree, drifts of snow curving up to the lower limbs, blocking her in. He had no clue how she'd ended up in there, but she was good and trapped, unable even to stand. He tested the edges of the drifts, checking for give. They gave all right. If he came any closer he'd find himself on top of her. And not in a fun way.

"Are you hurt?"

"My snowshoe's caught under me. I can't get up. I can't get out." The more she tried to claw her way out of the bowl, the more snow caved in on her, soft and impossible to maneuver through. She was swimming in snow up to her shoulders, branches whacking her in the head whenever she got some momentum going from her sitting position.

"Are you warm enough? Can you feel your toes?" She appeared to be decked out in jeans and a short, trendy ski jacket, although it was difficult to tell by the way her clothing was packed with snow. She looked more like a human snowman than a smart Canadian prepared for all weather.

Women. Her need to be fashionable probably had her legs close to frostbite, if Jack Frost hadn't already been nipping at them.

"Get me out of here!" There was panic stitching her voice, and when Josh failed to move, she scrambled, making her situation worse.

He balled up the knitted afghan and tossed it under the branches that protected her from the worst of the wind, afraid to come closer. "Wrap yourself in that."

"JC! Get. Me. Out."

She struggled again, but the snow was like quicksand, grainy and loose, ready to pull her down each time she stirred. He was going to need more supplies. A rope. Shovel.

"Hang tight. Don't try to get out." He didn't wait for her reply, but ran back through the snow, his feet falling through at various depths, sending him off-kilter like a newborn fawn learning to walk on ice. He needed to stay calm, slow down, make a methodical plan to get her out of the shifting snow. A twisted knee wouldn't do either of them any good.

Before long the light he'd hung on the clothesline came into view. He moved it to a nail in one of the porch posts and untied the line. He grabbed the shovel he'd used earlier while fixing the generator, and figured if he couldn't get Simone out of her bind with this he'd come back for reinforcements—waking the entire cottage if necessary.

Back at Simone's tree he carefully tested the edges of the drift again, backing off as soon as it began to crumble. Then he lay down on the snow, wondering if the clothesline would be long enough to haul her to safety. If he had to dig her out, how long would it take in conditions such as this?

"Simone?"

"You left me here!"

"Don't get your frozen lace panties in a huff. I had to get supplies."

"How do you know they're lace?" He voice was indignant and he chuckled, trying to shake the vision of her lovely shaped buttocks encased in delectable, fine fabric designed to make a man crave all it hid from view.

He tossed one end of the clothesline to her, reminding himself to cool his jets. It wasn't a good time to be visualizing her wearing close to nothing.

"Hold on to the line and I'll pull you out."

As soon as she tugged, the rope cut through the drifts. "It's not working," she complained.

"I know." Making sure he was on a solid crust of snow, he stood and grabbed the shovel. "I'm going to have to dig you out." He batted what looked like purple yarn out of his way, but it kept blowing back at him. "What is this?" It was wrapped around one of the branches, threaded out into the dark night, hooked on something else.

"It's my string."

"For what? Knitting?" A few feet from the edge of her drifts he began digging through the hard crust, hoping to make steps of some sort. But as soon as he broke through the surface he faced the same grainy pebbles of snow encasing Simone. One false move and he'd find himself in a similar predicament.

"It's my lifeline." What was she talking about? "To follow back to the cottage from the outhouse."

"You should have woken me."

"You were sleeping." Her voice was stubborn, petulant despite its tremor of fear.

"Quit moving. You're making it worse."

"I almost got out that time."

"No, you didn't. You're working against me and it's going to take longer if you keep that up."

"Then hurry. I can't get out—my leg is stuck under me. I can't undo the buckle."

"I'm trying." He scooped crystallized snow out of the hole he'd dug. It was no use. It was all deep and grainy under the thick crust. He needed to get creative. Fast.

"Hurry."

"Have you already been to the outhouse?"

"No," she moaned. "And I can barely feel my thighs."

He began shoveling faster, hoping to uncover a miracle in the snow's depth while he tried to form other rescue plans in his mind. She began trying to help again, only drawing more snow into her shelter. She needed to listen to him, trust him. Josh stopped digging, battling his frustration.

"Why are you stopping?" she asked, her voice low with worry. "Don't leave me, please, JC. I'll promise you whatever you want. Just don't leave me to freeze. I'll—I'll set up your friend with distributors or other designers. Get her a discount on ribbons. Anything."

She still didn't believe he'd made the accessories. That cut.

He sighed, still resting against the shovel despite the way the wind nipped at his exposed cheeks. "Do you want me to help you or not?"

"Get me out." Her chin was starting to vibrate despite her obvious fight to keep her teeth from chattering.

"Yeah?"

"Please!"

"Then do as I say and stop trying to climb out!"

"I'm not a weak damsel in distress. I can help, JC."

He couldn't see her in the darkness under the branches, but in his mind's eye he pictured her with her hands on her hips, ready to do battle.

"Would it kill you to accept help? To admit that you can't do this on your own?"

He shone the flashlight in her direction, seeing her silhouette under the spruce as she began scooping snow, trying to break the crust that worked as a barrier between her bowl and where he'd started to dig. More snow piled in on her and she shuddered as it seeped around her waist.

She didn't learn, did she?

"And is that better?" he snapped. "Doing it yourself is working out fine for you? Shall I head inside and wait for you in front of the nice cozy fire?"

"I'm not going to just *sit* here." She was getting close to hysteria. Panic. On the verge of losing rational thought, which meant she was in an even worse state than she'd let on.

Josh quickly moved south several feet and dropped the shovel at his feet. He stretched himself out over the crusty snow, wondering if he was taking a stupid risk that would cost them both. As he slithered forward, testing the drift's edge, he talked to her in a calm, soothing voice, using her name to help her anchor her thoughts. "It doesn't make you any less of a powerful woman to accept help when you need it. It's a sign of strength, Simone."

He held his breath for a count of three, ensuring he was speaking without judgment so she'd relax and not allow panic to drag them both under.

She began trying to kick her frozen legs, pushing herself closer to him, snow shifting and pouring down her side and likely into her coat. She struggled harder, scrambling to reach him.

That did it. No more Mr. Nice Guy. "You know why people like you die in house fires, Simone?"

She didn't answer.

"Do you?" His voice was harsh, commanding.

"No, I don't flipping know. I'm not in the mood for a pop quiz right now. I'm freezing."

Below the anger he could hear the tears in her voice. He pulled the shovel up to his side, turning it so the scoop was extended to her, his grip firm on the handle. If she sat on the blade he might be able to drag her up over the loose stuff and onto the crust.

"They die in house fires," he said calmly, snapping the shovel out of her reach so she'd focus on him, "because they're too damn self-reliant to accept help when they need it."

She lost control of her shuddering.

"Grab hold. Sit on it, lay on it, whatever you can do, just get your weight on the scoop and hug the shaft—you'll be steadier that way."

She hesitated, likely put off by his tone, until he said, "Do it."

Her eyes met his in the thin sliver of light from the flashlight at his side and she tentatively placed her mittened hands around the shovel, stretching to do so, the blanket still wrapped around her higgledy-piggledy.

"Hold on as tight as you can and don't move a muscle."

She wrapped her arms tighter.

He gave her a nod to check that she was ready, then tugged her toward him. Her legs slowly straightened like a pulled-out accordion and the shelf beneath Josh began to buckle. Carefully, he wriggled backward, inching Simone out, drawing her like a sled over the soft snow.

She tried to help by kicking her legs, the large snowshoes flopping and catching on the drifts, tilting her sideways so she almost fell off the shovel's blade. He halted her movements with a harsh, "If this had been a house fire, you would have just died, as well as put my life in danger by trying to do it your way. Don't. Help."

She allowed him to haul her the rest of the way out as though she were a dead fish, then help her stand on her snowshoes. She looked weak, half-frozen, and he worried that she hadn't actually finally acquiesced to him being in charge, but that, rather, she might be two seconds away from becoming a human ice cube.

"I thought you were going to leave me," she said, her teeth chattering uncontrollably.

"You are pretty stubborn." He watched her for a second. She was in no shape to trying wrangling the snowshoes over the uneven drifts. Picking her up, he carried her in the direction of the outhouse before deciding that was a death mission. He turned, heading back to the cottage.

"You'll relieve yourself in a bucket back inside where it's warm."

She didn't fight him and he picked up his pace, worried about her lack of pep.

They landed on the back porch sooner than he thought possible, and not pausing to take off their boots or outerwear other than her snowshoes, Josh placed Simone right in front of the fireplace. He knocked the biggest chunks of snow off her, then carefully placed two logs on the dwindling blaze and yanked her chair as close as he dared. The blanket he'd tossed to her under the tree was caked with snow and he discarded it before pressing his bare hands against her skin, assessing the level of chill.

Her cheeks were icy and her fingers so cold they wouldn't be able to undo her snap or fly. He hurried to the kitchen and plugged in the electric kettle they'd used for hot toddies, before returning to her side. "Should I wake the girls?"

She shook her head, stopping him when he leaned back to holler for help. He eyed her for a split second before agreeing with her decision. She might be too embarrassed to call the others, but he knew what needed to be done—and waiting for anyone right now could cost Simone dearly.

He took her bare hands and slipped them under his sweater, instinctively jumping back at the frigid touch. She tried to pull away, but he held her gaze with a shake of his head.

"We need to take off your jeans. The snow packed into them is going to give you frostbite, if it hasn't already. Plus when it melts it's going to keep the cold against your skin."

"I'm okay," she said, fighting the chatter of her teeth and momentarily winning, before they began rattling again.

"No, you're not. I make the executive decisions. If I say you need something, then that's what you're going to get, you hear me? This isn't a game where you win independence points. This is life or death."

He freed one hand from hers, tipping her chin so she'd be forced to meet his gaze. "Do you trust me, Simone?"

She didn't answer, seeming so small pressed against him, so vulnerable, lost and in need of direction. Not just with her clothing, but with her life.

"Do you trust me to make that call for you?" he asked.

With tears in her eyes, she nodded.

"Then we need to take off your pants."

JOSH'S HANDS WERE LIKE fire against her numbed skin. Every sensation was as intense as though she was being singed by live wires. She wasn't sure if it was the cold that had taken over her flesh or Josh's gentle, careful touch.

He released the button of her jeans, his fingers tugging down her zipper before gripping the waistband and shucking off the denim in one swift move that left her quaking in the fire's heat. He pushed her onto a chair, then pulled the inside-out pants over her ankles. Thank goodness she'd shaved her legs that morning. She knew this wasn't the time to think about those sorts of vain things, but she was a single woman hopped up on hormones and he was a hot specimen of manhood stripping her with single-minded determination. Not thinking about the state of her legs would be like the prime minister not thinking about politics.

"Your feet stayed relatively warm." He ran his hands over her feet, ankles, calves, up to her knees and thighs, assessing for frostbite, and she wanted to slip off the chair and into his arms. She felt exhausted and colder than she could ever have imagined, and wanted to suck in his strength and warmth like a hungry vampire.

Vulnerable. That's how she felt. But she felt safe with JC and trusted him to take care of her without fuss or drama. It surprised her, but it was Josh she wanted stripping her in front of the fire, encouraging her to take a sip of warm tea, wrapping a blanket around her as he moved with swift confidence, setting her up for survival.

As much as she hated to admit it, there were some things men like JC were great for and right now he was doing it. He was rescuing her and she needed it. He neared recklessness in his haste to stoke the fire, and she set her pride aside and listened, obeying him with a submissive compliance she didn't know she was capable of. She hadn't treated him in a way she was proud of, and yet, no questions asked, he was taking care of her with an efficiency that didn't leave her feeling helpless. In fact, she almost enjoyed it. He wasn't leaching her power or strength, he was simply caring for her, carrying the torch when she couldn't.

He held a hand in front of her to test the heat radiating from the roaring fire.

"Can you feel the warmth?" he asked. "At all?"

She thought about it, then shook her head. "Not much."

He grabbed her chair and yanked her back an extra foot. "Don't move closer. Not yet."

She wasn't sure whether she was still clutching the blanket over her bra or not, her hands had gone so numb. She still had to pee, but knew she wouldn't be able to go without JC's help. She could hold it a bit longer.

"I thought you were going to leave me out there." Her voice sounded small, broken, and a tear slipped out.

JC squatted in front of her, his expression serious and definitely worried, which made her tears that much harder to hold back. "Do you really think that poorly of me?"

Yes.

No.

But when he'd disappeared after she'd been such an independent cow, she really wouldn't have blamed him if he'd left her there. She'd truly believed that if she'd just gotten the angle right she could have crawled out. However, she knew now that she would have frozen by then.

"I'm sorry."

"You were cold and stuck."

"And a bitch," she whispered.

He smiled, but didn't agree, and she loved him for it.

"If that had been a house fire I would have cost us our lives," she said, taking all her strength to acknowledge how wrong she'd been.

She resisted the urge to reach out and touch him, to let him know without words that she trusted him, appreciated him. Saw that he was special. He was a decent man and probably one of the best.

Just not the man she needed. Not a man she could get along with for the rest of her life. But maybe they could stop fighting and be friends.

"You okay?" JC brushed his thumb across her cheek. She barely felt his touch, her jaw struggling to hold in the chatter that kept shaking her body. "Does anything hurt?"

She shook her head. *Only my pride. And sense of self. I used to believe I was a nice person.*

But the way she'd treated JC the night before, she knew she had some growing up to do before she had her baby. It wasn't right to lash out at someone just because he made her experience things she didn't feel strong enough to handle.

He tucked a hot water bottle from the kitchen behind her back and took the chair beside her. The heat of the bottle felt amazing. He leaned over to brush her cheek again, wiping away tears.

"I'm not really crying."

He lifted the cup of warm tea, but pulled it back when she reached for it. "No." He tucked the blanket tighter around her body, then held the mug to her lips, refusing to allow her to help. "Sip."

The warm liquid felt good and she sipped more, watching JC. Eventually, he shifted closer and lifted her feet from under the blankets, tucking them under his sweater as he had with her hands. He sucked in a sharp breath when her soles hit his abs, but kept her feet against him, wrapping his palms around the tops. "Do you feel this?"

She nodded. "My feet are okay."

"They're pretty cold, too. We've got to start slow—you might have hypothermia. And if you do, you'll soon feel something, although I doubt it will be pleasant. Tingling, pain. It's all normal."

Something fun to look forward to.

They sat in silence, his heat seeping into her, slowly reducing her shivers. JC was careful to warm her without infringing on her space, and she half wondered if he was afraid to use skin-to-skin contact. Not that she blamed him. She hadn't been all that nice to him, going as far as to imply that he was gay. She didn't know what it was about the designs and why she couldn't acknowledge that he may have made them. She supposed it would mean that she'd have to reassess her old perception of him—a thought that scared her even more than the attraction that simmered between them.

In due time he pushed her chair aside, as well as his own, and pulled the couch a few feet from the fire. He helped her move to the cushions, the new spot chilly in comparison to the old one even though it was just as close to the flames.

"Do you still need to use the washroom?"

"Can I warm up more first?" The thought of having to move away from the fire was less than appealing.

"You sure?"

She nodded. She could hold it a little while longer.

JC yanked his sweater and T-shirt over his head in one fluid move, leaving him bare chested. Her breath caught in her throat at the sight of all those toned muscles rippling as he created a nest of blankets around them on the couch. What was he going to do? Press his advantage and go for skin-on-skin? She didn't know whether to feel shy, be ticked off or enthusiastically remove her lingerie in anticipation.

Instead, he simply tucked her into a ball, pulling her shins against his chest, slowly providing more heat as she huddled in the nest of blankets.

"Did you really make those things that Tigger was looking at on your phone?"

"Even the candy-apple red ones. Are they any good?"

Simone paused, unsure. If she complimented him would it go to his head? Would he become arrogant and ignore her opinion because he felt as though he was already at the top of his game and just needed to be discovered?

"Be honest," he said, displaying a genuine need to know.

"I'm fairly certain you already know they're exquisite." She pulled the blanket up under her chin, edging her butt closer to him so she could steal more of his heat. This going-slow thing sucked. She wanted to press the length of her spine against his chest and have him wrap himself around her.

"Do I have talent?"

When she seemed reluctant to answer, he added quickly, "Be a straight shooter. I need to know."

"And what if what I say goes to your head?"

"Everything goes to my head—don't you know my type?" While his tone had a sharpness as though he'd been insulted, she knew he was joking, trying to break down the barriers they'd erected over the past day. Despite herself she laughed. The man was a piece of work. So persistent and determined. Traits she definitely admired and valued. Traits that had gotten her into hot water a time or two herself, when she'd let hers shine.

"You have some serious talent. You could go far with this. But..." She paused, making sure he was still listening. "It's going to take a lot of hard work and you're going to need to fine-tune your color sense and possibly a few other things. Competition is fierce and there's no room for 'good enough.'"

He nodded, his expression serious.

"What?" she asked softly.

"How do you know if you're ready?"

"You jump in."

"No testing the waters?" He gave her a quick look of assessment, his forehead tight.

She shrugged.

"Nothing about you is quiet or understated, is it?" he asked, his voice low, almost admiring. "Bold and beautiful."

She felt heat flood to her face. He'd just called her beautiful. And meant it. And not in a "you're beautiful and I want to bed you" kind of way, but in a cherishing one. That was new. She liked it.

"Thank you," she said, unable to meet his steady gaze. "But I believe you mean strident and overly confident. Maybe even pushy and annoyingly outspoken, as well."

He laughed quietly so as not to wake the others. "Yeah, that, too." But instead of raising her hackles, she found herself laughing along with him. What was it about this man that allowed him to slip under her barbed wire, anyway? It was as though they understood each other on some level she hadn't even known was possible. Made a connection.

"So?" he asked, when the rich sound of his laughter died away. "You really think I could do something with this?"

"Yeah, but it doesn't quite fit your image."

"Tell me about it," he said with a groan.

She leaned forward, pressing into him more fully when a cold breeze seeped under the blankets, making her shiver. "I think your image might be inaccurate."

They shared a look, and with a tremor of anticipation she realized she was about to ask him to warm her, skin to skin.

Chapter Nine

Simone woke up clinging to a bare chest. She pulled her cheek off the warm skin to a magnificent view of a sleeping man. Ho, ho, ho. Merry Christmas to her.

She closed her eyes again, at war with herself. She loved how JC felt, protecting her with his body's heat. But she hated the way she wanted to run her hands down his tautly muscled skin. Her fingers wrapped themselves in the tuft of chest hair between his pectorals. It was a slightly darker color than his head of hair, more similar to his jaw's stubble. She shuddered, still slightly chilled from her stupid outhouse adventure. She'd ended up relieving herself in an old plastic tub, JC disposing of it over the veranda's edge for her so she wouldn't have to go out in the cold. Humiliating and disempowering didn't even begin to touch what a blow that had been to her identity as an independent, self-reliant island unto herself.

But the worst blow was that she didn't even care that she wasn't this big, tough, do-it-herself dynamo at the moment. She wanted to just cuddle up and let him deal with everything.

Which meant she must have frozen her brain under that damn tree. How stupid was she, not testing the drift's edge while tying her yarn to the branch? One minute she'd been standing there, the next moment she was slipping under the spruce, snowshoe folded under her, dug into the snow, trapped.

What would've happened if JC hadn't woken up and come looking for her? Still, she couldn't imagine a world where she'd willingly wake up JC in the middle of the night so he could accompany her to the little girls' room.

A large hand covered hers, holding it still.

"That hair is attached, you know."

"Sorry." Her fingers flew open, releasing their grip.

"Are you warm enough?" JC's voice was rich, deep, and gravelly in all the right ways, sending tingles down her spine. She leaned away before realizing that her lacy bra was rather see-through. She pulled the blankets around her, leaving JC's rock-hard chest exposed.

Her flesh felt chilled without his body pressed against hers.

JC sat up, tucking the blanket more fully around her shoulders, allowing her to take it with her as she climbed off the couch and practically into the fireplace. He must have melted, sleeping that close to the flames.

She reached for her phone, touching a button to wake it. She had to take her morning shot in an hour and ten minutes. Not much time. Plus she'd slept in. Everyone had. The cottage was eerily silent without the howling wind rattling the place.

"Merry Christmas," JC said. He was stretched out on the couch, his hands tucked behind his head, watching her, his chest tempting and bare.

Was he really a good guy? He'd been so kind last night. A thoughtful, caring gentleman who had allowed her a semblance of dignity while taking charge in a way that didn't leave her bristling. He hadn't made her feel weak or powerless—at least not intentionally. Anything that made her feel less strong was because she had been fighting imaginary battles with a very decent man.

His words echoed in her head: *It doesn't make you any less of a powerful woman to accept help when you need it. It's a sign of strength.*

Maybe it wasn't so much about it being a sign of strength as accepting help from the right person. A person whose hand up would give her strength, not diminish it.

"Merry Christmas," she said softly.

"What time is it?"

"Time to go." She pulled on her dried jeans, keeping the blanket hunched over her shoulders for privacy. Next, she grabbed her sweater from where it was laid out on a chair. She dropped the blanket, back turned, not caring what he saw, since he'd already seen enough. She pulled her hair out of the sweater and let it hang down her back, adding another layer of warmth.

Fully dressed, Simone brushed aside the curtains on the French doors and peeked out. It was calm and still. A beautiful white Christmas, and it wouldn't be long until the helicopters came.

She felt the warmth of JC standing behind her. She resisted the urge to cave against him, to suck in his strength and heat. Turning, she found him much too close. She had to get home and create a baby. She had plans, plans that didn't involve him. He was wonderful, but he wasn't The One.

She raised her hands to create a barrier, her heart skipping and racing unsteadily as her fingertips grazed the smooth skin of his pectorals. He had a six-pack and a teasing line of muscle that slipped under the waist of his low-slung jeans. His body represented heady doses of power and sexy masculinity, and she needed to tell her hormones to stand down.

JC ran a thumb over the edge of her jaw, sending shivers straight to her core. "How are you feeling this morning?"

"Good. Fine."

She pulled away, feeling as though she'd bared too much to

him last night. Too much skin, too much longing. Too much vulnerability. Too much everything. She needed space to think. He was going to ask her to feel things about him, before turning around and deciding, too late, that she really wasn't his type, after all.

"I guess you're off the hook," she said, feeling a foreign pang of disappointment. She went to duck past him, but he reached out and lightly grabbed her by the waist, holding her, making her desperate for his touch.

"I'll be down on the ice digging out my machine. But I won't leave Nymph Island until I know you're safely on your way and this damsel in distress is no longer in need of my rescue services."

Simone straightened as if someone had goosed her. *Damsel in distress.*

She'd allowed his help and now he was throwing it in her face. She had known it was coming; why had she let her guard down? She braced herself, waiting for the next blow. Waiting for him to prove without a doubt that her first gut reaction in regards to who he really was had been correct.

"You're still having that baby?" he asked.

"Does it matter?"

"You should wait."

"Why?" she asked, chin raised. If he was suggesting she wait and have a baby with him, he'd lost his mind. They'd spent most of the past twelve hours butting heads.

"Because. You might...regret it."

"You think I don't know my own mind?" Her head cocked dangerously to the side.

"I think you do," he said carefully.

"You don't like single moms? You have a problem with them?"

"I think we've proved I'm a helluva lot more open-minded and accepting than you are, Simone Pascal." His voice was soft, his face close to hers, fencing her in, not allowing her to lash out and escape.

"Yeah? Then how come you can't let me be? Why are you always in my thoughts? Why are you always making me doubt my path? Why are you always there to see me fail? I'm strong, dammit."

"I know," he said softly.

"I'm strong! I'm independent. I don't die in house fires. I can take care of myself, but I can accept help, too. I'm not who you think I am. I'm more than that."

JC yanked her close, kissing her so deeply she had to cling to him to keep from falling to the floor. Their anger was like fireworks, electrifying and exploding around them. She curled into him, shaping herself to his build, wrapping her arms around his neck, hating the way she absolutely loved kissing him, hating the way she wanted all of him. Every bit, from his attention and admiration to his heart.

No. Not JC. She couldn't fall for a man like him.

"I am not a damsel in distress," she said, breaking away.

"Don't have a baby."

"Don't tell me what to do." If they got together, this would be how it went—him in the driver's seat. JC determining the who-what-where-when-why-and-how of her future, even when it pertained to her own body.

"It's a mistake. You don't know what you're doing."

"Oh, I think I do!"

"He's a stranger."

"That's the point. A stranger can't—" She cut herself short, not adding *hurt me, be disappointed in me, expect things I can't deliver.*

"What if he wants the rights to his child?"

"He's signed a consent."

"Laws change. He's a stranger and could carry—"

"He's been screened. Psychologically. Diseases. The works. That's a lot more than I get dating some guy I pick up in a musty old cottage." She dared herself to look down her nose at him, dismissing him even though it hurt every cell in her body to do so.

Men like JC couldn't give her what she needed. She knew that. She'd learned that lesson already and wasn't going to test the theory once again by breaking her own rules. Not for him. Not for anyone. She couldn't trust him and she couldn't trust herself around him. If she wanted to carry her own baby she needed to get JC out of her life—pronto.

"What if your child has a hundred siblings from this guy? Do you know what kind of mess you're inviting into your life? There are other ways. You're an amazing woman, Simone, and I know how much your independence means to you, but sometimes you have to consider the things you may have overlooked. You have to contemplate the people you never thought of."

He could *not* be asking her to consider him. He just couldn't.

Don't even go there, she warned herself silently. *Stay angry. Don't let him see you cry. Don't let him open the cracks. Don't even think about how serious he might appear at the moment—he's just bothered that the chase is over and he didn't win.*

"Yeah, well, nobody has stepped up." She flung herself away from him as other occupants of the cottage awakened due to their loud exchange. "And quit bossing me around. Just because you got to play hero..." She shook her head, not trusting her voice.

"Simone—"

"No." She turned away, then whirled back to face him. "I don't want you and I don't need you. So just step out of my life."

"Simone—"

"I thought you were different. I was obviously kidding myself because you kiss like you mean it. Like you're someone I could get close to. A man I could trust."

"I am someone you can trust. Have I ever hurt you?"

"I need someone who will support me without telling me what to do with my life."

"I'm not looking to run your life, Simone, just stride along beside you. Be your copilot."

"I don't *need* a copilot! Just because you make me hot in my panties—I mean warmed me up with your hot body... God*dammit*. You know what I mean." She pressed her fingers to her temples. What was it about this man? "I don't choose you." Her voice was wobbly, tears threatening to fall. She needed to run. And there was nowhere to go. No escape.

She pulled herself together, reassembling her protective walls, chin raised once again.

"You might as well leave now, as I won't be requiring your services," she said coolly, stopping herself from adding *ever*. "Have a nice Christmas."

She turned her back and began straightening the living room, ignoring the Summers who were peeking out of their bedrooms with concern. Simone, for the sake of the future she had planned for herself, hoped she never saw JC again.

THAT WOMAN WAS COLDER than last night's blizzard. How had he allowed himself to believe she wasn't going to turn against him, and that her softening last night had been her letting him into her ice palace to help melt the walls that surrounded her heart?

He was stupider than a sack of hammers.

Josh stomped over the crusted drifts of snow between the cottage and his snowmobile down at the lake. She couldn't even take a joke, she was wound so tight. He'd been teasing, trying to compliment her and let her know that he believed she was strong —stronger than he'd thought—for allowing him to take charge last night. He'd known how difficult it must have been for her to set her pride aside, and he'd been stupid to think it had something to do with him.

He'd been a fool to believe that the moments they'd shared under the blanket had changed things. He'd felt something when he'd held her tight against his bare chest. A connection. And she'd felt it, too, but what did she do with it? Turned around and shoved it in his face.

He'd actually begun to think they might have something real, something he could take with him into his new life adventures. Someone who would have his back and actually understand him and all his messed up and confused ways. Someone who could see through all that and love him just the same.

What a fool. The worst of it was he'd known better, but had still plowed ahead, wanting to be wrong about his assumptions.

She was still the same old Simone his wiser, younger self had avoided in the high school hallways. She didn't do vulnerable and didn't like men who had a soft side or exposed her own. She was cool, calculating, and always on top.

She wouldn't change—not even for him.

He reached the lake and cursed. There were a multitude of drifts by the boathouse, but no snowmobile in sight. Which meant one of the mounds was his machine. He broke a branch off a nearby tree and used it as a probe, poking snowdrifts until he came across something unyielding. He began digging, his anger fueling him to make short work of the job.

As he brushed snow away from the controls, sounds of the Summer family came closer. He glanced up to see a group of them chatting and laughing, Simone trailing behind, her mittened hands shoved deep into her coat. She looked cold and miserable.

Good.

He turned back to his machine. All he had to do was start it, let it warm up, and he would be out of her life forever.

Not quite soon enough, but it would have to do.

He sat on the frozen seat and turned the key. The machine groaned and shuddered, indicating something was definitely wrong. He flipped open the hood to find that the wind had completely packed the engine with snow, likely part of its starting issue. Freaking Canada. Freaking winter. Why didn't he move south?

He began clearing snow from the engine compartment. The last thing he wanted was to be rescued and have to share a seat on a helicopter with Simone.

The men started clearing a spot on the ice for the helicopter to land, their cheery laughter snaking its way to Josh like a slap across the face. They hadn't been stupid enough to fall for an ice queen—and that's what he'd done last night…fallen.

Dammit.

He knew better than that.

"Won't start?" It was Evander, standing over the machine, looking impossibly large. Josh nodded, feeling defeated. Evander tried a few things, but the engine still didn't catch. "Too cold, maybe?"

"Yeah. Think so." His mother would be disappointed he wouldn't be able to take her for their annual Christmas Day snowmobile ride, but she'd survive. The frigid overnight temperatures likely had left the oil as thick as fudge, which meant his snowmobile wasn't going to start without a significant heat-infused intervention. One he couldn't provide out here.

"There's an extra seat in the helicopter. We'll come get this later." Evander placed a hand on Josh's shoulder, directing him farther onto the ice. The sound of helicopters grew in the distance as they made their way to the gathered group. Josh hoped the choppers landed quickly, as he was in no mood to chat.

Maya came hurrying through the thigh-deep snow from the woods as though afraid she'd be left behind. "I just threw up!" she announced.

"I told you we should have packed the pasta salads in more snow. Now she's got food poisoning," Melanie said, turning to Hailey. She located Tigger. "How are you feeling, little monkey? Are you okay?"

Hailey was tapping the back of her hand against Melanie's arm, studying her in a way that made Josh turn to study her as well. She didn't look pale. In fact, she was glowing, beaming at her sisters.

Uh-oh.

Josh quickly checked Simone, who, judging by her expression, had yet to clue in as to why Maya had been ill.

Hailey squealed, arms extended as she trundled through the snow to hug her sister. "This is so exciting! We're going to have cousins the same age!" She hugged her sister even tighter. "They'll be in the same class at school. Same with Daphne's baby!"

"Wait, what?" Melanie asked, as Daphne got in on the hug, as well. "You're pregnant?"

Connor paled and Josh reached out to steady him. "Congratulations, man."

Connor gave a jerky nod and blinked twice before a ghost of a smile stretched across his face.

Simone quietly joined the celebrating sisters. She offered congratulations, but Josh could tell she was struggling with the news. He wanted to provide comfort, to let her know that it was okay to feel everything that had to be storming through her—

even though it would mean she'd reject him again. A woman like Simone not only deserved a good man in her life, she deserved support, love, and acceptance.

Which was probably why she was choosing to have a baby on her own. Unconditional, uncomplicated, reliable love.

He shook his head, the realization seeming so obvious. But before he could figure out what to say to Simone, Evander called to the men, "Are we all clear?"

They'd knocked down the few drifts on a patch of ice the wind had blown fairly clear, to make a semi-decent landing pad.

The guys who had gathered around to offer the newlyweds their congratulations nodded.

"We should be good," Finian said.

Evander waved in the first helicopter, like the former navy commander he was. Then he turned away from the incoming machine, arms out, shepherding the women closer to the boathouse, encouraging them to face away from the soon-to-be-driving snow as the rotors kicked up the grains and whipped them their way. "Get low."

One of the choppers landed, while the other hovered nearby, waiting its turn on the impromptu landing pad.

Josh reached down to shelter Tigger, then picked her up, bundling her across the snow to the waiting rescue party, protecting her the best he could from the kicked-up snow. He placed her inside as Evander helped usher the women in.

Josh caught Simone's eye. She looked sad, tired, and rejected, which was odd. He was the one who'd been rejected. Soundly.

He shook his head, knowing he had to stop thinking about her, stop wasting his time on a done deal. She would never allow him to help in the ways she needed the most.

Evander closed the doors and gave them a pat, providing the

pilot a thumbs-up through the glass. Josh caught one last glimpse of Simone fidgeting with her mitts, her dark eyes cast down. He reached for the door, but Evander pulled him away, the machine already lifting off.

It was time to move on. Without her.

Chapter Ten

Simone had been bustling around her mother's kitchen all afternoon and their Christmas dinner was finally ready. Her mom hadn't tossed her cookies since the night before, but she was still pale, clearly worn-out from her battle with the bug, and dozed on the couch with a blanket tucked under her chin.

Simone cupped the dish of mashed potatoes, loving the way the heat seared her palms and radiated up her wrists. Since being stuck under the spruce tree over twelve hours ago she had been craving heat. Lots of it. She was wearing layers of sweaters and had spent extra time checking the turkey just so she could allow the oven's heat to wash over her. She still couldn't get warm, but she knew it wasn't a physical affliction as much as missing JC's steady presence. Not just his body's warmth, but the fire in his eyes when he battled with her and the way he didn't allow her to walk over him. Quite plainly, and as annoying as it was, she missed the way she heated up in his presence.

But she didn't need him and he'd only mess with her plans, while breaking her heart.

She poked the steamed carrots with a fork, testing if they were done, her mind drifting to the firmness of JC's chest. The way his hand had enveloped hers when she'd been tugging on his chest hair, his body snugged up just right beneath her. She flung the fork onto the counter.

Damn him. Damn Josh Carson to hell. He had managed to get under her skin—and good. She'd walked in her door right on time to take her hormone shot, but instead of injecting it, she had gently laid the needle back in its case, unused.

She still didn't know why, only that it felt like a betrayal to carry a baby that belonged to another man.

Which was messed up.

No, it was beyond messed up.

It was crazy. Plain and simple. A baby was her plan. Possibly her last chance. She had the father chosen. The appointment for insemination was booked. She'd rearranged her *entire life* around this appointment and now she couldn't go through with it because of a stupid kiss in a stupid enchanted cottage.

She'd wanted to be swept away by someone on Nymph Island for so long that she was tricking herself into believing that what she'd felt with JC had been real.

She knew better than that. Just because he seemed to know when she needed someone to give a little push back, or turn her toward the truth so she couldn't avoid it, didn't mean he was the answer.

But right now, no matter what the pros and cons list kept telling her, a baby didn't feel like an answer, either. And a child wasn't going to make her feel any less alone.

Thinking about JC was a colossal waste of time. He wasn't going to give her a second chance. He wasn't going to come running to sweep her off her feet and have a family with her. She was too high maintenance. Too hot and cold. She'd been a bitch and turned his gentle ribbing into a barb, then lashed out at him and stormed off without even a goodbye.

She removed her apron and tossed it aside, bracing herself

against the counter, head hung low. She should have taken the hormone. She could still take it—it would just be much later than usual.

Grabbing a blank notepad out of her mother's junk drawer, she started marking the paper with vicious lines, trying to draw through her frustration, seeking that quiet place within her where she usually found answers.

Realizing she was refining the designs she'd thrown in the fire —the very designs she'd promised herself she'd abandon in order to focus on her new life—she flung the pages across the counter.

No more. No more ideas. She needed to focus on what was coming up on her horizon. Her plan. No more split focus, no more chickening out. She'd take the next hormone shot in the morning and hope it worked this month.

She opened the email app on her phone, looking for items to delete without reading. Coupons, spam, jokes. Gone, gone, gone. She didn't want to think right now.

Why had it felt so good to be rescued by Josh? Why had she loved being warmed by his body? She'd known he'd only been joking that morning about her being a damsel in distress, but nevertheless he'd struck upon that hidden cave inside her where she kept all her fears locked away.

Her phone rang in her hand and she nearly dropped it. It was her father. Were they supposed to talk again today? Twice in twenty-four hours seemed like a lot.

"Merry Christmas," she said crisply.

"Merry Christmas," he replied.

Silence stretched over the phone. Apparently that was all he had to say.

She bet this would be just like any relationship she had with JC, because he was just like her father. The pressure to do better, to change, to impress him, to do a song and dance every time she wanted his affection. She needed to be self-sufficient and never need him. Ever. When she'd needed her first business loan she'd gone to the bank, not her dad. And yet...and yet last night she'd kept turning to JC. She'd had other options and she hadn't chosen them. Why?

Because JC wasn't her father, was he? She didn't have to be featured in the *Financial Times* to get a get a crumb of approval. JC thought she was strong just the way she was.

"Do you have hobbies?" she asked her father.

"You know I like to play golf."

"I mean, ones I don't know about. Maybe crafts, puzzles, model building? Some men build stuff."

"Are you okay?"

"Do you?" She was holding her breath, waiting.

"It's a waste of time and money. Real men build real things. Useful things." There was a slight pause before he asked, "You didn't get me any of that crap, did you?"

"No. I sent you a gift card."

"Right. I saw that. How's your business?"

No thank-you? JC would have thanked her. She was certain of it.

"I sold it."

"You what?" Thomas sounded incredulous and she secretly enjoyed the feeling of having pushed him off center.

"Don't worry, I got a good deal," she said drily.

"The whole thing?"

"Everything." A feeling of panic welled up inside her. She'd sold her livelihood and wasn't having a baby.

Wait. She wasn't having a baby? Since when? And what the hell was she doing if she wasn't having a baby?

"Do you have something new on the line?" her father asked.

"No." Her voice sounded small in her own ears.

She could do something with the plus-sized teen designs. She could help JC—be his consultant. She wasn't completely gone, was she? She still had a chance to reclaim her old identity. She wanted that, right?

"You're pregnant, aren't you?" her father accused. "What's his name?"

"I'm not pregnant."

"Then who the hell has got you acting like a fool?"

She *was* a fool, but only because she'd let JC get away. She'd hurt him, then pushed him away, rejected him before he could reject her.

"I'm tired of working so hard for nothing."

"Those who work hard get ahead. Welcome to life."

"And then what? I'm ahead. I'm not happy. I don't have a family. A boyfriend. I have everything but I have nothing."

"And a boyfriend is supposed to fix that? You're being irrational."

"Maybe my whole life is irrational. I made money thinking I'd finally get your approval, and guess what? I didn't get it. All I got was more pressure to keep working and earn more, get more accolades. And I did. And so what? I'm still the same person. I still have the same problems. Only now I'm tired, I'm alone and I'm not happy." Her voice was wobbling and she despised the way she was breaking down.

JC had seen her unhappiness. Why couldn't her father?

She really needed to stop comparing the two.

"Maybe you weren't meant for this."

"Are you suggesting I'm not strong enough? Because I am. Nobody else I know has gotten as far as I have in such a short period of time."

JC had told her she was strong. That asking for help was a sign of strength. She'd let him help her and the world hadn't caved in on her.

She swiped at the tears streaming down her face.

"Simone, listen carefully."

"Why?" She sounded bitter, resentful. "I listened to you my entire life and here I am."

"Yes. Here you are. With enough money to change your life. With the knowledge that you went out and took the business world head-on and won."

She drew in a deep, unsteady breath. Stupid logic. Stupid issues making his words sound like praise and approval.

She forced herself to continue listening and not hang up the phone. He was going to get her all wound up and rushing off in the wrong direction again, wasn't he?

"You're the strongest person I have ever met. I pushed you so hard because I believe you can change the world."

Her designs. Those stupid designs. They just wouldn't leave her alone.

Because they were game changers, that's why.

Wait. Her mind rewound his words. He thought she was the strongest person he'd ever met? How did that happen?

"You can get anywhere you want, Simone. You can have all those things nobody else can achieve."

She pulled her earlier sketch closer, assessing it for potential, allowing herself the freedom to feel the fizz of excitement as more ideas came to her. She paused, then flipped to a new sheet, allowing her pencil to fly, uninhibited by her internal business mind, which demanded that the designs reach a wide audience, be simple and cheap to make, and be on trend.

She had something with this line of designs—her originals. She really did. Something bigger than she'd had yet.

But did she still have the energy to make them happen?

Did she even want to? What if they took over her life? What if this was still the wrong path for her? She didn't want to spend the next decade chasing her own tail right back to where she was in this moment.

"You can't give up now."

"Yes, I can."

"You're destined for great things, Simone."

Here comes the pressure, in three, two, one...

"But maybe I pushed you too hard."

Simone's mouth opened and closed, she was so shocked by his admission.

"And you're right. You have achieved great things. I haven't shown it well, but I *am* very proud of you. You solve problems and you don't cause them. But I still don't understand why you're giving it all away."

She considered making a joke about money talking, but settled on the truth. "I'm tired. It's fun and I love making designs, but the pressure to make something super huge out of every idea is onerous. It's taken away the joy." She lowered her voice. "I want to take some time off, but I feel guilty and like I can't because of the way you treat me." She pulled in a deep breath, afraid to say everything she felt, but knowing this might be her only chance. "I need you to not pressure me. It's not healthy and I push myself hard enough as it is."

"Okay," he said simply. No pause. No anger. Just acceptance.

"Okay?"

That was it? After decades of him pushing her to work harder, longer, smarter than everyone else, he was letting her off the hook? It was like gearing up for a hurricane, battening down the hatches, struggling against the gale force winds, only to have the storm come all the way up your walk to drop dead in your doorway.

"As much as I want success for you..." Her father paused, and Simone had the feeling he might be struggling with emotion, something she had never witnessed before. "...I want your happiness more. Do what will make you happy. Just tell me what does and I promise I will do my best not to interfere or push you in the wrong direction."

"But I don't *know* what makes me happy," she said, her voice wobbling once again.

"Then go find it. Push down every door and look behind it. When you find it, seize it. You have time, health, youth, and now wealth on your side. Get out there. Find it. Own it."

Brushing the tears from her cheeks, Simone thanked her father in a whisper.

"I'll always be proud. There is nothing you can do that will ever take that away. Now get off the phone and go figure out your life." There was a hesitation as though he'd almost hung up, then figured he should add, "Merry Christmas."

When he hung up for real, Simone laughed, sniffing back tears.

Dammit, her asshat of a father was a pretty damn good guy. He might even make a decent father for her upcoming sibling.

Which meant Simone probably had to rethink everything.

She looked around the kitchen at the cooling dishes of food, and peeked into the living room, where her mother was gently snoring. Simone folded the dress design, tucking it into her purse. Maybe she didn't need to reject her designer side entirely. Maybe she could sketch for fun, see where it took her—if anywhere. She had time to take a break, connections if she didn't want to produce and sell the designs herself.

A baby could wait, couldn't it? Maybe her uterus would come out unscathed when they removed the cysts and ovaries, and she'd still be able to carry her own baby. Maybe a surrogate would be okay, too.

Out of habit, she opened her email again.

How was she going to find happiness, though? How was she going to break the habit of working only on ideas that would lead directly to prestige and success? How was she going to let herself be a loose ribbon in the wind? An artist. A designer. Nothing on the go but a license to explore her own creativity, her own life.

Her breath caught in her throat, the possibilities overwhelming.

Read more email. She needed more distractions.

An incoming message caught her attention. One of the MOM members was looking for someone to collaborate on hair accessories for their toddler line.

The project had JC's name all over it.

SIMONE WAS CRYING OVER AN email. Outright bawling. Ugly crying at its finest.

She ran to the upstairs bathroom and locked herself inside, smothering her face in a towel in hopes that her mother wouldn't overhear her self-pity fest of sorrows and confusion.

Her sobs racked her body, her ribs aching with the force of her release.

Her tears turned to hiccupy laughs as she fell on her butt, stunned by the realization that she had been lashing out at JC's creations because she was jealous. He had the freedom to create whatever he wanted without thought to market, cost, or trends. Anytime he wanted to he could sit down with his supplies and let his heart lead him. He was living his life and taking the risk, and making something that he obviously loved to create.

The ridiculousness of a multimillionaire, well-known designer being jealous of a man with a boxful of ribbons and a glue gun was so inane she had to hold her sides against the giggles that overtook her. Her lashing out at him hadn't entirely been about her feelings or insecurities, it had been about *work*.

And her getting off track with her life and dreams hadn't entirely been her father's fault. It had been hers. It was her life, her call to make.

Simone stood suddenly, dropping the tear-soaked towel in the tub.

Her new life plan came to her in a flash. It was so simple. So elementary. She was going to follow her heart. She was going to play and discover what truly made her happy.

She'd pull a JC and follow her heart and talents. That man was as genuine and real as the pope, but all she'd allowed herself to see was the alpha side she so despised because it reminded her of her father.

She'd blamed that aspect of Thomas's personality for pushing her with unrelenting persistence, driving her to do better, climb higher—and further away from her own dreams. But in the end, it wasn't just him at fault, because she possessed that trait, too. And it had caused her to push away JC, caused her to do damage.

She opened the bathroom door, mind made up. It was time to find JC. Time to repair things.

"YOU HAD US SO SCARED," Josh's mother said as she cleared the table from their Christmas dinner. Their palpable relief when he'd shown up via helicopter that morning had left him feeling humbled as well as loved.

Not like with Simone. He doubted she would have shed a tear if he'd fallen through the ice or if his chopper had gone down.

They hadn't spoken or even made eye contact when their flights had landed near town, depositing them by the group's vehicles parked in a frozen marina. They'd simply gone their own ways, Evander and Tigger giving him a ride the rest of the way home in Evander's truck so the sisters could drop Daphne off first to ensure Santa arrived before the little girl.

"I know, Mom. I'm sorry," Josh told her.

"We're glad you're all right, son," his stepfather said, giving his shoulder a squeeze.

"Me, too. I'm sorry I worried you," he said again.

He began washing dishes with Polly in the kitchen while their parents moved to the living room to curl up in front of the fire, pausing to kiss under the mistletoe along the way.

"How will you get your snowmobile back?" Polly asked.

"I'll probably drive out with my truck in a day or two. If I let this cold snap pass it might start on its own."

He dried the gravy boat, thinking about the island. About Simone. She'd admitted he had talent. Potential.

He leaned against the counter, facing his sister. "What would you say if I told you I make frilly hair accessories for little girls?"

Polly began laughing. She hunched over the sink, her hands limp in the sudsy dishwater. She caught sight of his expression and straightened suddenly. "You're serious?"

"Sadly."

"Is this why you've been acting strange lately?"

"Probably."

"Okay. But I don't get it. This is a secret?" She handed him a large casserole dish to dry.

"There's still stuffing on it," he complained, handing it back.

She stuck out her tongue and plunged the dish into the warm water again, swishing it about before handing it back. "You know, a good drier would have taken care of that."

He licked the spot where the stuffing had been stuck. "Like that?" He rubbed the tea towel over the spot, drying his saliva.

Polly's nose scrunched up and she flicked water at him from

her fingers. "Get a new tea towel and give me that dish." She made grumbling noises as she rewashed it yet again. "You're such a brother."

He smirked.

"Did you get a new tea towel?"

He balled up the used one, chucking it at Polly, who ducked, her perfect hair missing the chance to get mussed up. He grabbed a new towel from a nearby drawer.

"And don't you think I didn't notice you changing the subject with your shenanigans." She gave him a stern look. "Why is your hobby a secret?"

A hobby. That's all it was, but he wanted it to be so much more. He wanted it to become his identity. Something he could be proud of. As gutsy and scary as that was.

He let out a slow breath, his shoulders lowering in increments. If he wanted to take his "hobby" up a notch, he needed to talk to Simone. Which was, oh, let's see...the last thing on his list of things he wanted to do. Ever.

"You know who you need to talk to?" Polly asked, shaking a soapy finger at him.

He cringed. *Don't say it.*

"Simone."

She'd said it.

"She doesn't believe I'm capable of creating the accessories. Or if she does, she thinks I'm gay."

Polly sputtered, choking with laughter. "And what would ever give her that impression?"

"The items are rather feminine."

"Show me." She held out her hand as though he could somehow procure one.

"My phone died, but I think the burn unit may have photos on their website."

"The burn unit? In Toronto, where you volunteer?"

"Yep."

"Interesting." Polly assessed him as she dried her hands on her woolen slacks, an uncharacteristic gesture. She reached into her nearby purse, pulling out her phone.

"How are things with you and the ex?" Josh asked, as she brought up the web page.

She lifted one shoulder noncommittally. "I want money. He doesn't want to part with it. Hate is an ever-expanding emotion. That about sums it up."

Her long fingernails slid across her phone screen, tapping intermittently. Her head tipped to the right and her expression softened, a smile tugging at her lips.

"These?" She held out her phone for him to see. He nodded. "They're beautiful. And obviously much loved." The expression on her face reassured him. She saw the beauty in the creations as well as how they brightened the days of small children. A win-win. But he wanted to do more. He wanted to reach further, touch more lives.

Polly put down the phone, hands on her hips. "You need to talk to Simone. For real. These are amazing."

"Thank you."

"Do it," she insisted.

"Right now?" he joked.

"Just tell her I sent you and she'll help you until the world ends."

He was pretty sure he'd discovered the loophole on that claim.

"She's connected," Polly continued, turning back to the dishes. "She'll know everyone you need to meet in order to make this a go. Seriously. Talk to her."

"Right now?" he repeated, still joking.

"Well, she's probably having supper with her mother."

"Her parents are split up?" he asked, trying to disguise his interest by polishing the blade of his mother's old carving knife. It had been a wedding gift from her first marriage, to Patrick/Patricia, and it always made Josh think about those confusing times when his mom had tried to support her partner the best way she could, but finally had had to go separate ways when Josh's father went through his metamorphosis into womanhood.

"They split up when she was a teenager. A real piece of work. Always pushing her to do more and work harder. I remember her winning an award for top marks and he asked her why she hadn't got 100 percent. The look on her face..." Polly paused, her mouth pinched with anger on Simone's behalf. "I'll never forget it. She was crushed. But the next year, what did she do? Got 100 in math."

"Does she see him much these days?" Josh felt as though he was close to something.

"I think they talk on the phone."

He waited for her to continue unloading her peeves about Simone's father. Josh's patience was rewarded when his sister turned, still ticked off. "Nothing was ever good enough and he made her work harder and longer than everyone else. It's no surprise she's as successful as she is, but I don't think it came without a price. She keeps telling me she wants an understanding, touchy-feely guy, because she can't keep a man longer than about five seconds." Polly laughed. "But a woman like her? She needs someone who's determined and can stand up to her, or she'll walk all over him without even realizing it."

Josh nodded in agreement.

"She just needs someone awesome, you know? A guy who will support her and encourage her without pushing so hard or taking over with his own ideas. There has to be a point where enough is enough, and good enough is good enough. Everyone wants to feel as though they've made their parents proud. I don't know if she's ever felt that."

So good ol' Simone was fighting ghosts, not him. Josh had sensed that, but had still allowed himself and his own ego to get in the way.

She was strong, but afraid of failing. She feared not being enough for those who cared about her, hence her practice of always giving the Summer sisters dresses, which must take inordinate amounts of time. She had a father who pushed her to do well in her field and what had she done? Sold it all.

That woman was about as lost as a blind man reading a paper map.

It was time someone told Simone Pascal that she was special, amazing and most of all, enough. Enough for him.

As long as she thought he was enough for her.

Polly wiped down the counter, then faced him. "So? Are you going to talk to her and get some advice?"

"Yeah." Josh reached for his coat. "And I think I'll do that right now."

Chapter Eleven

Josh never did find Simone on Christmas Day. Nobody had come to the door at her mother's house or her own. By then, out of leads, he'd lost the steam behind his mission to convince Simone he was her man, and had ended up going home.

That had been three days ago, and he was feeling more and more miserable with each hour that went by and he hadn't figured out an amazing "we're meant to be together" speech that would knock down her walls so she could fall into his arms once and for all.

Josh pulled into the grocery store parking lot, having spent the entire afternoon bouncing through Lake Rosseau's drifts. He'd reclaimed his snowmobile from Nymph Island, winching the dead machine up onto his truck. He was hungry and ready to indulge in a hot barbecue chicken, potato salad, and a couple beers in front of tonight's hockey game with his favorite teams, the Boston Bruins and Toronto Maple Leafs.

He would not spend the night thinking about his projects.

And definitely not thinking about Simone.

Not tonight.

Parking toward the back of the lot, he trudged through the couple inches of wet, heavy snow that had fallen during the day. Shoppers were struggling, the snow-covered asphalt causing their carts to become unwieldy machines. After watching a woman in a red parka unsuccessfully shove hers through the mess, the front wheels digging in and tipping the cart forward every time she got momentum, he finally gave in and went to help. By the time he reached her, she had come around to the front of the cart, puffing as she tugged it forward.

He hesitated for a second, then picked up the cart and carried it.

He felt entirely unprepared to face Simone despite the baker's dozen speeches he'd rehearsed in his head over the past few days. All he had to do was open his mouth and start talking, but the only thing he could think about was how cute her thighs looked peeking out from under her bulky coat and how pale she seemed, with dark circles smudged under her eyes.

"Where's your car?" he asked.

She pointed across the lot to a black SUV that looked as well kept as the woman who drove it.

"Have a good Christmas? Get home in time?"

"I caught my mom's flu. It's left me wiped out."

He set the groceries inside her vehicle, pausing as he tried to think what to say.

"Thanks," Simone said. "And I wanted to..." She glanced up, a battle happening behind her eyes. He took a step closer, not wanting to miss a single word that came out of her plush lips.

"I knew it!" A male voice came from behind them, causing Josh to tense. "I always *knew* it."

Polly's ex-husband, Chuck. Not what he needed right now.

Simone's shoulders drooped and she turned to face the man, but Josh ushered her into her vehicle.

"Go. You don't look like you're in the mood to deal with a severe case of dick-itis today."

A small smile curved her lips and she shot him a grateful look.

He pulled her seat belt out of its retractor, handing it to her. She didn't even balk at the help, which buoyed his hopes.

"I always knew it," Chuck said, drawing alongside Josh.

"Have a safe drive home, Simone. If you need anything, I'm always running to the store."

"Okay."

Josh looked back at her in surprise, having expected an argument.

"When Polly told me about your latest venture—your gay little hair accessories—everything finally clicked," Chuck said.

Josh sighed and screwed his eyes shut, summoning the strength to hold back what would surely be an immediate desire to sock the man in the jaw. For some reason, the urge to prove his manhood didn't surface. There was no flare of anger, no flash of need so intense he found himself pummeling Chuck's ugly nose. He opened his eyes to find Simone staring at him.

How about that? He might actually be okay.

Maybe being different didn't always mean pain or anger. And yet he'd seen so many people get hurt for letting their freak flags fly.

Was it because Josh finally didn't care what others thought? That he realized those who attacked were often those who were unfulfilled and weren't following their own true path? Was it because he knew that his new business was truly him and that if he followed it he could make a difference in the lives of others? Did being secure in his sense of self negate everything else?

Maybe this was why Patrick/Patricia never fought back or engaged in self-defense.

"You're just like your dad," Chuck said. Josh winced, feeling the cut of the blow on his father's behalf. "Or whatever he is now that he's had his balls chopped off."

Josh felt the familiar urge to strike, the desire to protect

Patricia flaring inside him. But he kept his back turned, absorbing the support he was silently receiving from Simone of all people. He gave her a tentative, what-can-you-do smile, not sure what was going on in her head.

Her quiet curiosity had turned to the brightness of dawning comprehension.

Great. Just what he needed—her pointing out the fact that he seemed to be having his own gender issues with his new career of choice.

She slid out of the vehicle and into his arms, surprising him. Her lips landed on his, hot with want, kissing him in a way that would turn Sir Elton John straight.

She released Josh, ignoring Chuck. "You're a good man, Josh Carson." She tapped his chest almost playfully. "Don't forget to remind me to discuss that deal with you for your accessories. I think it's going to become *huge*." She placed a gloved finger over his lips when he gave her a confused frown, then slipped back into her vehicle, shutting the door and starting the engine.

What deal?

Oh, dang. She was covering for him, building him up, making Chuck squirm with the hint of possible success raining down on Josh.

Simone Pascal had his back.

He grinned. The kiss had been pretty good, too. Although kissing her always felt like the most natural, real thing he'd ever done. And would like to do again. And again.

There was something about that woman.

There really was.

Damn, he was going to fall even deeper in love with those bossy pants of hers if he wasn't careful.

Wait.

Love?

Aw, crap. He was doomed, wasn't he?

And couldn't be happier, because she'd kissed him. By choice. Even if it was simply to shut up Chuck.

Things were definitely looking up for a certain Josh Carson of Maple Avenue. Yes, indeed.

Josh turned to the silent man beside him as Simone drove away. "Sorry. What were you saying?"

"Wasn't that Simone Pascal? She doesn't date just anyone, you know." Chuck sized him up. "Last I heard she was dating one of the Toronto Maple Leafs. Is she trying to get you to go straight?"

All right. Josh had had about enough. He stood a little closer, allowing his size to intimidate as he moved into the man's space. "I've been meaning to talk to you. Polly says you're having issues getting the divorce papers signed on time."

"Oh. Well, I...I need to discuss things with my lawyers."

"What's the holdup?" Josh clenched his hands into fists, squaring off.

"I'm sure it will get all straightened away in the new year. Holidays, lawyers, you know how it is."

"I'd hate for my sister to be held back in any way. If by February she isn't free of you, you'll start answering to me." He smiled, thinking that maybe his old identity of being a troublemaker wasn't so bad to have on hand.

"I—of course."

"Good. Happy New Year."

Josh left the man standing in the middle of the lot. As he headed into the grocery store, doubt started to seep in about the intent behind Simone's kiss. She didn't seem like the kind of woman who took favors without repaying them. Was she trying to level the score for the way Josh had saved her back on Nymph Island? If so, he was going to have to find many more favors to do for Simone. Many, many more.

SIMONE FINISHED CURLING HER eyelashes, then layered on the mascara. She leaned back and studied the effect. Her eyes were smoky and sultry, her dress hugging her in all the right ways, tucking in below her ribs before flaring out over her hips. She slipped on heels that emphasized the length of her legs and, using her curling iron, placed a loose curl in a wayward strand.

Good enough. She checked her watch. Fashionably late.

She would definitely catch the eye of JC at Polly's New Year's Eve party. Simone wasn't proud of the way she'd left him on Nymph Island on Christmas morning, but their grocery store encounter had been pretty decent. Her only regret was how she'd had to make such a hasty exit after that steamy kiss, in order to play out her ploy to make Chuck jealous of JC's new venture.

Gay?

She knew JC wasn't. And now she felt doubly bad for tagging him with the term when he'd obviously dealt with that sort of thing enough, given his father's own gender issues. But the poor guy was going to have a tough time proving he was still a macho man after he went public with his accessory business. A smoke jumper making delicate, pretty hair ribbons for little girls. It was sweet and she loved him all the more for going for it.

She wasn't sure where she stood in JC's world, and hoped he'd come to the party tonight so she could talk with him. If that didn't work, she'd force herself on him with business plans and lists of connections.

She drove to Polly's house, knowing the Summer sisters were due to arrive around the same time. She half hoped they'd already be there, half hoped they weren't, so she could talk to JC without them interfering.

Polly took her coat at the door and ushered her into the ginormous house she used to share with her husband. Music was playing in the living room and her tasteful Christmas decorations were still up. The scent of cinnamon wafted from a nearby row of candles and Simone wondered where everyone else was.

"Am I early?"

"Perfect timing," Polly replied.

Simone hated being the first to arrive at parties, although in this case it might give her a chance to catch up with her friend.

"How are things going?" She'd noticed that the more masculine décor items seemed to be missing from the house, which meant Chuck had likely experienced the full boot since the last time Simone had been over, a few months ago.

"Pretty good." Polly smiled as though she had a secret.

"Who is he?"

"What do you mean?" Her friend frowned, tucking her white cardigan tighter around her thin frame.

"The man who has you smiling?"

Polly let out a bubble of excited laughter. "Oh, he's nobody. Nobody yet, anyway." She raised her eyebrows, grinning. She led Simone into the dining area, where an appetizer feast had been beautifully laid out. "Make yourself at home. Nothing is off-limits."

"Other than the man who has you smiling? Name, please?"

"Maybe he's not for *me*."

"Oh, no. Don't you dare set me up with someone." *Especially if he's not your half brother.* Simone stepped toward her friend as though she could stop her from causing havoc in her life.

The doorbell rang and Polly gave her a teasing grin before hurrying to the entry, where the door was already opening. "Josh! Happy New Year."

Simone felt a rush of nervous energy rush through her, sending her thoughts into a tizzy. She wanted to run out the back door so she wouldn't have to face to JC, but at the same time she wanted to run up and kiss him like there was no tomorrow. She quickly poured herself a glass of wine, knocking it back. She refilled the glass, then, muttering to herself about acting cool and calm and most of all collected, she joined the others in the entry.

JC, who had just hung up his ski jacket, allowed his gaze to slowly linger over her. Unapologetic, hungry, but reserved. Totally JC. His attention paused on her glass. He met her eyes, knowing exactly what the drink meant.

"Are you here alone?" he asked.

She gave a coy shrug of her shoulders. "The night's still young."

"Allow me to top up your glass," he said, placing a warm hand at the base of her back, sending rivulets of desire coursing through her bloodstream. He curved his body protectively around hers, guiding her to the kitchen when the doorbell rang again, as though worried someone might steal her away.

She loved where this night was going already.

"I'll just get the door," Polly said, clearing her throat.

"I think I forgot to thank you for your help at the grocery store the other day. With my groceries and with Chuck," Simone said to Josh as they entered the kitchen.

"I should thank *you* for rescuing me from him."

She turned to him, placing a hand lightly against his chest, then backing off, the heat from their touch too distracting.

"I mean it." She regarded him through her lashes. "Thank you. For *every*thing." She knew she was being vague. Nevertheless, his head tipped, acknowledging her intent.

She let out a sigh of relief. No digs. No machismo.

Instead, JC gave her a wicked grin, full of mischief as a hint of scorching desire flared through his blue eyes, making them darken. "Have I mentioned I have a soft spot for damsels in distress?"

No. Just no.

She told herself to cool it—that he was simply testing her. She knew she had some pretty explosive trigger points, but that still didn't mean he should push them.

"You know I'm teasing, right?" He sounded worried and his hand drifted up to her shoulder, giving it a light squeeze. The move was reassuring and her head drifted toward him as though pulled by a magnet. He massaged her shoulder, his free hand adjusting a loose strand of her hair so it stopped tickling her chin. He moved closer, his aftershave sweet and spicy. She trusted him, knew he would never intentionally hurt her and that she needed to let go of her issues—for him. For them.

"Do people never tease you?" he asked.

"Not if they want to live."

"You need to know that I tease because I care." He was nuzzling her curls now, and she was having issues with breathing and rational thought as well as keeping her wineglass upright. "If I didn't like you, I wouldn't tease you." She tipped her head, offering her neck with a moan as the heat of his breath traced a line up her flesh to her earlobe.

"So your enemies get off easy?" She leaned into him. "Nice."

He laughed, his breath tickling her ear.

Simone stepped from his embrace to refill her already full glass and JC slipped in behind her, his hands gliding around her waist. She found herself leaning against him yet again. What kind of game were they playing? They had unsettled business to discuss before they moved down the path they were on.

She spun in his grip and he stepped back, probably thinking she wanted him to let go. If only he knew how much she craved his touch, his steady presence.

She held her glass between them as though in protection and he took it, wrapping his hand around hers, trapping her fingers momentarily as zings of her body's approval sang through her. The hormones—even a week later—must still be in her system.

Or else it was simply the impact of having a steamy hunk of male standing in front of her with a whole lot of carnal desire flickering in his gaze. She'd love to run her fingers over his abs again, only this time without numb fingers so she could feel every ridge of muscle twisting under his skin as her touch led to reactions within him.

"Simone?"

She dragged her attention away from his crisp dress shirt, waiting for him to continue, but his sister entered the room, her body language apologetic as she fetched beverages for more arrivals.

JC, gaze locked on hers, set her glass aside.

"Josh, can you do me a favor and show Simone the new bedspread in the guest room?" Polly turned to Simone. "The color combination is exquisite. I could totally see you creating something with those tones. If you need the quilt for inspiration, feel free to take it home with you."

The woman moved away, picking up a previous conversational thread with her guests before Simone could protest the setup. Oh, Polly was good.

"Not at all awkward," JC mumbled in amusement as he led the way.

"Well," Simone said, pushing away her nervousness, "I did want to talk to you in private." They turned down a hall, the sound of music growing fainter. "Why does your sister call you Josh and not JC?"

"Nobody other than you has called me JC since high school. Hard to believe, but I did grow up and move away from my troublemaking days."

Another dig, well deserved, but a dig intended to keep her and her assumptions about him in check. On Nymph Island she'd been so intent on holding him at bay that she hadn't even noticed everyone called him Josh, leaving her the only one stuck in the past. She hadn't given him an equal chance—well, any chance at all, if she was going to be honest about it. She had judged him based on her own insecurities and issues, as well as his past. Hardly fair. And time and again he had proved to be more than that.

"Do you prefer to be called Josh?"

He nodded.

As they passed a small table laden with various ceramic Santas, Simone quickly turned, sliding her palms up Josh's chest to prevent him from continuing forward. It was time to apologize. It was what she had come for.

He bumped into her, snatching her waist to steady them. Awareness shot through her as their bodies pressed against each other. She took a deep breath, suddenly feeling nervous about her plan of putting herself out there. She wanted Josh, didn't want this feeling to end, but was afraid that he'd reject her if she allowed herself to be vulnerable.

"Is this private enough?" he asked, his voice low and rough with something that made Simone's pulse pound in anticipation of something delicious.

She nodded, glancing over his shoulder at the vacant hallway. He deftly snagged her by the wrists, pulling her against him as he pivoted to pin her against the wall.

"You look like you want to bolt," he said gently. The length of his hard body was pressed into hers and she finally felt as though she could breathe, think straight.

"I'm not having a baby."

Okay, that wasn't how she had planned on starting the conversation, but it was a definite icebreaker.

His grip loosened ever so slightly. "Why?" His expression

lightened, his eyebrows suddenly raised in understanding. "Oh, the flu?"

The flu wouldn't have interfered with her appointment, but she loved that he was thoughtful enough to consider that.

"No."

He tilted his head just so, his blue eyes full of curiosity.

"You were right."

"I was?" Another lifted eyebrow, and words spoken slowly, as though he was wanted to avoid a trap. No gloating. Just concern. If he kept that up she was going to cry. Nobody had worried about her since she was a kid.

"There are—were—a lot of unknowns," she said carefully.

"Such as?" His thigh was pressed to hers, holding her in place, causing her body to keep fumbling for the mind-shutdown switch so it could play.

"It doesn't matter," she whispered.

"It doesn't?"

"Only that I decided it might be wise to give a real man a shot before I pulled the trigger."

She'd had a good long chat with herself and had decided to put insemination on hold so she could pursue things with Josh. She'd thought she wanted a baby, but really, deep down inside, what she wanted was love. While things were new and uncertain with Josh, she felt they had potential worth exploring. The ovarian cysts would still need to be removed, but she had a little bit of time to think, breathe, and live. In a few months she could reevaluate her baby plan as well as the idea of surrogacy for her frozen eggs, but right now it was time to explore love.

Josh said nothing, merely watched her for a moment, his Adam's apple bobbing with every swallow.

She laughed nervously. "That makes me sound as though I'm a certifiable man trap. I just meant that—"

He silenced her with a kiss. Her wrists were still encased by his hands, their arms trapped between their bodies as they angled their mouths, digging against each other for better access.

He broke the kiss. "Are you asking me to be your boyfriend?"

"Yes." She wanted to add about fifty clauses, but figured they could get to that later.

He studied her for a moment. "I know you're strong enough, but are you open-minded enough to date a man who makes frilly accessories?"

She gave him a wicked grin. "Make me your girlfriend and I'll show you things that will make you wonder why you ever questioned my open-mindedness."

SIMONE ADJUSTED HER DRESS and dabbed at her mouth, hoping to eradicate any traces of smeared lipstick. Because she was certain it was smeared. Everywhere. She bit her bottom lip so she wouldn't grin. Polly's bedspread had definitely been inspiring.

She giggled as Josh joined her in the hallway, tucking in his shirt. He slung an arm across her shoulders. "I'd say that opened my mind." He leaned into her, giving her temple a kiss. "So? Now what?"

She hooked her fingers in his, not wanting to join the celebration going on in Polly's living room. She wanted to ring in the New Year, but not with anyone other than Josh.

He leaned against the wall, legs splayed. He pulled her into the V, his hands loose around her waist.

"Believe it or not, I don't have a plan," she said.

"That must be new for you. Any heart palpitations? Sweaty palms?" he teased.

She leaned her hips against his, giving him a saucy look.

"Know what's funny about you not having a plan?" He gently

brushed a strand of hair off her forehead. "For the first time in my life, I actually have one."

"And what's that?"

"Take you to bed as often as I can."

She laughed, trying to escape his arms, but he tightened them, trapping her. She lessened her struggles, peppering his chin with kisses that gradually slowed as their bodies melded together.

"Seriously?" he said between kisses. "I'm going to go for it." He hooked a finger in the neckline of her dress, teasing her with a gentle touch.

She traced patterns down his chest, loving the hardness of his flesh. Next time she planned to spend a lot more time focusing on it with her lips and tongue. Maybe even a minute or two here and there to see what he liked best.

"I think you already did go for it."

Smiling, he bumped his forehead against hers, tracing her nose with his before planting a heavy kiss on her lips. "I may have to try again before the year is through."

"You have a few minutes and about a 90 percent chance."

"Not 100?"

"We are in the middle of a large party."

"That hasn't stopped us yet."

She felt herself blush as she placed a finger over his lips, loving the fact that they could tease playfully now without her getting bent out of shape. She trusted him. With everything. Including her heart.

He took her finger into his mouth, giving it a light nibble. Oh, yes. They were going to have a *lot* of fun together.

"So?" She shifted impatiently against him. "What's your plan?"

"I'm giving up firefighting. It was a big part of my identity, but it's time to see if I can make a go with my hair accessories."

He looked uncertain, as though this was the scariest thing in the world. A second later his features relaxed, and she could tell he had been waiting to take this chance for some time.

"Good."

"You don't mind dating a man who is..." His gaze shifted away and she knew he was struggling with how people would perceive him.

"Gay?" she teased.

His eyes flashed and he pushed her away. She waggled her finger at him. "Uh-uh! If you get to tease me, then I get to tease you."

"It's not funny."

"And neither is the whole damsel in distress thing. Your identity might be a macho male issue, but mine is being self-reliant and independent. If you knew how much it galled me every single time you had to bail me out—"

He shut her up with a kiss again, his hand drifting through her long tresses, cupping the back of her head. She had to admit she loved the way he took control. And he'd been right. She needed a man with big cajones. She needed *him*.

"I'll help you," she said when they broke apart. She placed another light kiss on his lips, wanting to stay connected with him, to keep savoring the way he felt against her—strength and protection but with a gentleness she craved.

Despite the way he was comfortable taking charge, she knew Josh would never infringe on her ability to remain autonomous. If she was down, he was up, and vice versa. He would be there, ensuring she met her goals, whatever they might happen to be. An equally strong and powerful partner who knew the rules of give and take.

Thanks to Nymph Island, at long last the man she'd always dreamed of was quickly becoming hers.

She gave him a grin. "Let's start by making a deal with Melissa's Cuties."

"Melissa's Cuties? For real?"

"You've heard of them? Good. Well, she's looking for toddler hair accessories and I think you'd be a good fit. Then we can talk about distributors, discounts, connections, and all that after we hammer out a contract with her."

"Are you taking charge of my life?"

"Yes. Do you have a problem with that?"

"No, but right now, more than anything, I just want you to be my girlfriend. Not my business partner."

"Are you really going to turn away this gift horse?"

"Until next year."

"Such a long wait," she teased, knowing they were only minutes away from midnight and changing their calendars.

"This year I want to be nothing more than your lover." She had to admit she liked the sound of that. "Next year we can worry about business, world domination, and hitting the cover of design magazines."

"Those things don't really change much, other than your bottom line, just increase the pressure to do it all again."

"And maybe after that, if we still like each other, we can venture into the undiscovered arena of domesticity and family."

"Are you proposing?" she asked, head tipped to the side.

"Do you think I should?"

"Well, I think it would be wise to show you all the ways I'm open-minded first."

"And I still have to show you all the ways I love you, Simone Pascal."

She froze against him. "You love me?"

He ran a thumb down the length of her jaw, sending tremors of desire through her. "What's not to love?"

"Overcontrolling, overconfident, strident..." She began listing the faults that had got her into trouble in the past.

"I happen to think those are qualities in the women I like to date. Plus I've noticed that you've been slowly letting me see your softer side. I like that, too. It all balances out quite nicely."

"How did I ever get so lucky?" She ran her palms down his chest. "I seem to have found a man who's real. Tough and yet—"

"Don't say it."

"I wasn't going to. And I love you, too," she blurted out, then closed her eyes in fear. Oh, God. It was too soon. Yes, he'd said it first, but it was still too early for either of them.

But she liked the way she lit up and felt alive when she was around him. She liked the way he took her to task and called her on her bullcrap. They had things in common and were strong enough and pushy enough for each other, and she loved that about him. About them.

Plus he was great with Tigger. Great with her friends. And he stepped in and rescued her when she really needed it. Dammit. Simone really, really liked it when he had her back. She didn't want to, but she knew she could trust him, love him, and not get hurt.

It was plain old out-of-control love. The one thing she couldn't plan for and the one thing she'd crossed off her list, thinking it would never happen.

Josh smiled, hugging her close. "Let's get out of here, shall we?" he whispered in her ear. She grinned up at him. She'd never heard anything better in all her life.

He tucked her against his side as they headed to the entry. From the other room came loud cheering and a chorus of, "Happy New Year!"

"Does that mean we have to talk business? Or can I still enjoy the early glow of being your girlfriend?" Simone asked Josh, disappointed that they'd missed their chance to ring in the new year in their birthday suits, bodies moving in blissful, wanton harmony.

"You can always enjoy the glow of being mine. Always." He twirled her around, catching her in the doorway, then pulled her into his arms for a long kiss. He pointed to a sprig of green above them. Mistletoe.

Love and mistletoe. Definite seasonal must-haves.

Christmas Eve
Nymph Island

Dear Santa,

Thank you so, so, so, so much for bringing me a daddy—he is writing this letter for me and I keep checking to see if he is writing all the words right. He says he is but I'm not sure because I can only read the beginner books because I'm just five and we aren't learning how to read very fast at school. It took you a really long time to get Evander for me (that made Evander laugh and smile. I had to tell him to write that part down) but he is very nice and he can lift me up in the air like I'm the whipped cream on top of a sugary sundae. It's like I can fly just like a fairy. But I'm not allowed very much sugar.

And Evander's going to be my forever daddy! Forever and ever and ever. And ever. He gave Mom a ring and now I get to hug him every day. Even when he's cranky about Mom not being careful about locking doors and checking her car mirrors. But there are no more bad guys because Evander scared them away. So it's okay to come to our house at Christmas tomorrow morning. Nobody will take my super bright fairy light that I asked for. Oh! I didn't ask for it yet. I asked for a pony in my last letter, but Evander says ponies in town aren't a realistic gift and that they don't fit on your sleigh, either. I secretly think Evander bought me one because he has lots of money and always finds a way to get things for me that I really like. So it's okay if you didn't get me a pony named Sparkles. Now I am writing you to say I would like a super bright fairy light for Christmas, please. (Mom says I must remember to say please.) (*Note from Evander: I already bought her the light, so no worries there, big guy. No pony, though. Maybe next year.)*

My fairies say they'd like new winter coats because the squirrels made them into nests again. Mom says that's what squirrels do in the winter and that they couldn't have known that they belonged to the fairies. Can you please make sure your elves put the fairies' names in the coats this time so the squirrels know that they belong to someone? The fairies names are still the same but Evander said I should write them down for you in case you don't remember. He doesn't know that you remember everything. He's an adult and he doesn't believe anymore. The fairies are Trixie (like the cottage's name), Ellspa, Vixey (like your reindeer Vixen), Tinkerbell (of course), Silverbell, Silvermist, Gillian, Fawn, Chippie (like the chipmunks I'm taming), and Periwinkle. I hope your elves have time but Evander says you are probably already in the air delivering presents right now. I told you he doesn't believe anymore. He can't remember your magic. Thanks, Santa! I know you'll bring good coats for my poor shivery fairies.

We live in a new house now. It's in Bracebridge with Evander and Granny Flo—that's Evander's mom who is a little bit sick. She's feeling okay though. MAJOR BIG NEWS! I'm going to be a sister! I didn't even believe it! It's going to take forever to be a sister. Months and months. I promise to be good and help out because I can't wait. I can dress the baby and do its hair and love it and squeeze it and give it a ride in my doll carriage. I won't feed it sugar and next Christmas I can help the baby write to you because I'll be big and will be able to write letters. More than just boring words like *cat* and *dog* and *mat*.

Evander is reminding me to tell you about the house because I got distracted. He's smiling a lot. I think he likes writing to you, too. (*Note from Evander: I do, actually.*) The house has lots of Christmas lights around the door and lots of trees and a big backyard. It's Evander's old house but he says you haven't been there in a really long time because he's all grown up now. I think it's silly that you don't come to his house now that he's big. Everyone needs Santa and gifts. Maybe then they would still believe and be nicer to each other. But Evander is nice even though he doesn't believe anymore.

In case you don't remember the house it's white and it's close to a park. It's not very close to my school though so my mom has to give me a ride on her way to go work on the island by our cottage. They are making a place for people to take a holiday that's not bad for the environment. It means that Mom and Evander have to talk about it a lot and it's very boring. Uncle Connor and Uncle Tristen like to talk about it a lot, too. Uncle Finian is okay though. He doesn't talk about it all the time. Only sometimes. He likes to talk about movies and movie stars. They are very pretty. He knows Ashley Judd—she was in *Tooth Fairy*. It's really funny. Evander says it wasn't that good and he'd only give it two stars but I would give it a thousand! I think Mrs. Claus would like it. You should get it for her for Christmas! And maybe some warm slippers so she can wear them when she watches the movie. That's what I do. She'll laugh a lot so don't give her anything to drink or it might come out her nose.

I don't have to go to the babysitter's very much anymore which is too bad. Evander showed me how to protect myself like I mean business. So I showed the boy who pushed me down and he stopped pushing me because he could see that I knew business now. We're friends sometimes except I don't see him. We go to different schools and not the babysitter's this year. My teacher's name rhymes with Walrus. It's funny because she's really skinny and doesn't look like one. She's very pretty like a Barbie doll. She thinks Evander is good-looking and a nice man. She says any woman would be lucky to have him. I told her he was taken and to back off because I knew business and I wasn't afraid to use it. I had to tell Evander five times to write that down! He doesn't write everything I tell him to like my mom does. He keeps asking questions and telling me I shouldn't tell you some things because they aren't what you put in a letter to Santa. Duh. He doesn't know we write letters to each other all the time and that I tell you *everything*. If you're friends with somebody you don't hold things back. That's what Mom says.

Love forever and ever. Write back soon and give Rudolph a snuggle from me. And rub his nose, too. He likes that lots.

XO
Tigger (Kim)

P.S. From Evander de la Fosse—Tigger's new daddy. Thank you for bringing light into my life again. I will always believe—despite what Tigger says—as well as believe in the power of love. Merry Christmas, big guy.

P.P.S. Don't eat the ginger cookies Tigger made for you. Her mother is trying to cut back on how much sugar they put in their cookies and it's not necessarily the best thing for ginger cookies unless you enjoy a lot of spice. I'll try to swap them out for chocolate chip ones before you come.

Hello Summer Sisters Readers!

Do you enjoy reading romance?
&

Would you like to be the first to hear about new releases from Jean Oram?
&

Do you love saving money on ebooks?
&

Do you want to get in on exclusive giveaways and FREEBIES?
&

If you answered yes to any of these questions you're going to love my author newsletter.

For fast & easy online sign up go to:
www.jeanoram.com/FREEBOOK

Love and Mistletoe Book Club Discussion Starters

1) Why do you think fighting fires is starting to mess with Josh Carson's mind and is causing fears? Do you feel these fears are normal or unfounded? Could it be an aspect of his personalty type or could it be situational? Why?

2) How did Simone Pascal evolve into the control freak she is at the beginning of *Love and Mistletoe*? Why do you feel she resists seeing Josh for who he really is? In what ways would seeing him for who he really is threaten her way of seeing herself and the world?

3) Early in the book, Simone resists accepting certain types of help from Josh. Do you believe she got over her personal hangups, or will they continue to interfere as their relationship (both personal and professional) continues to develop? How do you think her need for control will impact their soon-to-be intertwined professional lives? Will Simone learn to step back?

4) In which ways do you feel Simone and Josh are a perfect match (complement each other) and in which ways do you feel they are not a good match (bring out the worst in each other)?

5) *Love and Mistletoe* touches on some work/life balance issues that many successful women face. How did you feel about Simone's decision to have a child alone? Why do you think women choose this option? What do you think will happen in her future when it comes to family? (Feel free to expand the term 'family' to also discuss her father and upcoming half-sibling, as well as the Summers.)

6) What was your favorite part of the story and why? Share it with the group.

7) Evander was nervous about proposing to Daphne. Do you think most men get tied up with nerves when they're about to propose? Did you believe that Daphne might say no when she hesitated?

8) Do you think Josh's fears about revealing his hair accessory hobby were founded or unjustified? What do you think his firefighter buddies will say when they find out? Do you feel that his past experiences have impacted his fear of revealing his new to-be business?

9) Both Josh and Simone were being held back from telling others they were going after their dreams, causing many large and personal secrets that were founded in their fears. Do you think this often happens in real life as well? In what other ways have characters in the Summer Sisters series been held back due to fears? How did they get over them?

Did your book club enjoy this book? Consider leaving a review online.

The Summer Sisters Tame the Billionaires

One cottage. Four sisters. And four billionaires who will sweep them off their feet.

Love and Rumors ~ Love and Dreams
Love and Trust ~ Love and Danger
Bonus novel: Love and Mistletoe

The Blueberry Springs Collection

Book 1: Whiskey and Gumdrops
Book 2: Rum and Raindrops
Book 3: Eggnog and Candy Canes
Book 4: Sweet Treats
Book 5: Vodka and Chocolate Drops
Book 6: Tequila and Candy Drops (Coming Fall 2016)
Companion Novel: Champagne and Lemon Drops—Also available in audio

Do you have questions, feedback, or just want to say hi? Connect with me! I love chatting with readers.

Youtube: www.youtube.com/user/AuthorJeanOram
Facebook: www.facebook.com/JeanOramAuthor
Twitter: www.twitter.com/jeanoram
Website & Lovebug Blog: www.jeanoram.com
Email: jeanorambooks@gmail.com (I personally reply to all emails!)
Full book list—I'm always adding to it: www.jeanoram.com

I'd love to hear from you.

Thanks for reading,
Jean

Jean Oram grew up in an old schoolhouse on the Canadian prairie, and spent many summers visiting family in her grandmother's 110-year-old cottage in Ontario's Muskoka region. She still loves to swim, walk to the store, and go tubing—just like she did as a kid—and hopes her own kids will love Muskoka just as she did when she was young(er).

You can discover more about Jean and her hobbies—besides writing, reading, hiking, camping, and chasing her two kids and several pets around the house and the great outdoors—on her website: www.jeanoram.com.

Made in the USA
Charleston, SC
02 September 2016